Other works by Ellie Di Julio

The Hobnailed Boot of Tough Love
Anything But Ordinary

for mom and dad,
who taught me to love stories

inkchanger

Ellie Di Julio

Steeltown. A run-down city on the edge of the country, somewhere that can't make up its mind whether to be a perpetual sauna or walk-in freezer. The air is visibly grimy with decades of pollution smeared into the clouds, tinting the sunsets violent orange and neon pink. An emphysemic wind blows in off the rainbow-slicked bay all year, wheezing through the husks of years-deserted condos. Big Mamma Steel pulled up her sooty skirts and fled not too long ago, leaving her dependent children to wander and fend for themselves while she searched for blacker pastures. Those that could escape, did; now it's all old-timers reminiscing about the glory days and punk kids tearing themselves apart to escape the gravity of stagnation.

Crossing the rusted railroad tracks in the north end takes an unsuspecting townie directly into a no-rich-man's land, where they're accosted by panhandlers, buskers, and addicts. It's the diseased heart of the city, where those sadly lacking a mountain-brow McMansion scrape together the pieces that make up their short, brutal lives. Down here, under the unflinching gaze of the escarpment, abandoned buildings clutch entire communities of otherwise-homeless citizens, each wishing for a magic wand they can wave and charm life into making sense again.

At the intersection of most residential neighborhoods, you'll find a miniature version of the city itself in the ubiquitous corner stores run by immigrants who arrived seeking work and found nothing but deeper debt and new mouths to feed. No one there speaks much English, but they're fluent in the simple language of a loaded shotgun under the counter. Petty theft and assault has doubled and tripled since Momma Steel's hasty departure. It's amazing the "I'd never do that" things you'll do when money is scarcer than food.

Standing at the corner of Market and Hess, skirting the border between swanky downtown and lock-your-doors downtown, you'll see one of those c-stores, its fluorescent yellow glare too bright against the murky backdrop of smudged concrete apartments. The shelves overflow with every imaginable shade of neon packaging, every corn-syrup laced confection, every MSG-toting snack a 2 a.m. shopper could want. All the produce is spotted, the expiration dates are carefully blacked out, the doors are always open.

And if you peek between the lottery signs plastered over the plate-glass window, you'll spy two sketchy girls – one a short, blonde pear; the other a tall, dark wirebrush – getting ready to make a break for it.

They'd shopped here before. Okay, maybe not so much "shopped" as "shoplifted." Distinctions like that get murky at best when you're perpetually out of cash. Either way, you go home with groceries - that's what's important, right?

Zara slipped a dusty box of macaroni and cheese into the waistband of her jeans with practiced skill, flopping her oversized sweater over the bulge. The front pocket whispered as a can of chicken and stars slid to the side. She eyeballed the tantalizing display of Doritos but knew better; anything crinkly, no matter how delicious, could get you caught. And that meant going back to the state home, back to school, back to hell.

No one wanted that.

At the other side of the convenience store, Sofi lingered among the antique medicine bottles. A roll of toilet paper up each billowing hoodie sleeve made it harder than it should've been to pocket a bottle of aspirin; the pills rattled alarmingly as she tucked it away. Thankfully, her petite frame made it easy for her to slip behind the rusted shelves without being spotted in the convex ceiling mirrors. For the zillionth time, Sofi thanked whatever bedraggled deity watched over thieving street kids for inventing brain-dead adults that didn't install cameras.

The girls met up in the back near "feminine paper" and plastic utensils to compare notes, making sure they'd lifted everything they needed before nonchalantly strolling out the door. The five-high stacks of cracked pop carriers in the corner made a convenient impromptu conference table. It was their sixth lift at this place, and it had to be the last for a while. When you're stealing from folks, you have to give them a chance to restock and, more importantly, forget your face.

"Soup, pasta, coffee, meds, cookies, TP... I think we got it all," Zara whispered, ticking off the crumpled list.

Sofi patted her own pockets, double-checking her pickups and nodding. It was a light load, but you couldn't get greedy on a run. Too weighed down and you're too easily caught; they'd already lost some friends to juvy for that particular sin. Poor Scott and Tim – half a year in the slammer for a backpack full of gummy bears and candy bars. After that, everyone made sure to stick to the list.

"Let's get out of here," Sofi whispered. "I think 'This Korean Life' or whatever is over." She gestured towards the counter where the Asian shopkeeper sat hypnotized by her laptop.

They'd made it to the freezer-burned ice cream, nearly home free, when the office door sprang open behind them, revealing a shriveled old man clutching a Chinese newspaper. He was reading out loud, presumably to Counter Lady, nose buried in the text. When she didn't respond, he looked up to shout at her and spotted the girls. In a tense moment of contemplation, his eyes fell first on Zara, then on Sofi, then on their ridiculously bulging clothing. The instinctual algebra of the elderly rapidly calculated in his mind and told him these were a couple of no-good kids on his proverbial lawn. His face screwed up like a colicky baby's, then he started bawling at them in heated non-English so loudly that Counter Lady actually looked up from her screen.

Busted.

Newspaper Man lunged after Zara, but she had at least fifty years on him and wasn't worried. She whooped excitedly as adrenaline surged through her brain, like an energy drink dumped directly into her bloodstream. Her body shifted seamlessly into automatic as she leapt backwards, shoving over a rack of paper plates and plastic cups to cover her retreat. The owner swore angrily as he tried to untangle himself from the cheap wire shelving, the newspaper impotently flung in Sofi's direction in an attempt at slowing the girl down as she slipped into another aisle.

Zara rounded the end of the store, whooshing past the counter. Escape was only seconds away, and she simply couldn't help snagging two bags of Cool Ranch Doritos from the endcap as part of her grand exit. She yelled, "Fuck you, Mr. Miyagi!" over her shoulder, and sprinted out the door Sofi held open.

Together, the mismatched girls bolted down the store's steps, ignoring the face-slapping transition from air conditioning to early-fall heat, blindly rounded the corner, and darted up the street, putting on speed to make sure Newspaper Man wasn't on their tail.

Which is how they took down two well-dressed folks out walking their overly-groomed purse dogs.

Everyone crashed to the pavement, cans and packages landing with box-crushing force, leashes wrapped around ankles, a few minor abrasions, and a good deal more swearing than fancy folks usually indulge in. Adding to the chaos, the shop owners had scampered outside and had turned to hollering at one another only a few yards away over the protestations of dogs and people. The air clambered with noise; the street was filled with tangled limbs and snackcakes.

But not for long. The girls bounced up and scrambled to collect their loot, giggling with the headiness of escape mixed with the ridiculous sight at their feet. A particularly runny-eyed purse dog tried to rip a bag of beef jerky out of Sofi's hands, but Zara bopped the animal on the nose with a wad of unraveled TP she'd rescued. It let go, startled and greatly affronted, then tried nosing its owner into fighting for it.

In a renewed fit of laughter, much to the dismay of the tangled townies and the bickering store owners, the two girls raced off towards the railroad tracks, heading the complete wrong direction for anyone who had any sense.

Laughing and sputtering, they ran through the run-down, grey neighborhoods of the north end. Passing the nearly-new project housing and abandoned train station, they crossed from "this is a decent place to live" firmly into "you might get shot while getting shot" territory. The familiar route to the wrong side of the tracks quickly calmed their crime-addled minds.

Zara slowed to a walk now that the immediate threat of capture and being reamed out by an angry Asian had subsided. The buzzing halo of adrenaline still tickled her skin, the bounce in her step and grin on her face completely chemical. She tried to hang onto it as long as she could, knowing it would evaporate soon and leave her in the usual dull grey haze.

"You'd think that'd get old after a while," she puffed as she caught her breath.

Sofi hustled to fall into step beside her, panting heavily. Street life hadn't made her a better athlete, unfortunately. Running always winded her, and her carrying capacity had only just reached twenty pounds; not much better than the miserable failure she'd been in gym class. She was convinced she'd be a flabby wimp for life. If running from cops, dogs, and armed shopkeepers hadn't turned her into a sleek running machine by now, nothing would.

"Nah," she said between gasping breaths. "The thrill of the chase, the excellent rewards, the heroic homecoming – who gets tired of that?"

Zara smiled and shrugged. This was far from her first run, but the excitement never wore off. The zing of adrenaline pumping in her veins and the giddiness of pursuit was addictive. Zara had never done drugs, even after escaping from her last "home" and dropping out of school as a sophomore, but she knew they couldn't be as good as the sheer ecstasy of low-grade malfeasance. It made everything crystal clear; the tingle of it oozed down her scalp like honey, down her throat, and directly into her heart with a fire no brain-melting substance could ever hope to duplicate. It drove away the darkness. At least for a little while.

The girls threaded their way in silence through the first few fall-reddened trees and navigated alleys between boarded up, bowed row houses. They had been running buddies – not to mention roommates and fast friends – for the last two years, and when you've lived in close quarters for that long, there's not much to say when you're walking home.

A distinctive variety of silence grows between people who have mastered confidence built on knowing each other's secrets. It's nurtured by long, deep conversations in the dark, curled up in the same bed; it's cultivated by breakdowns and intimacy; it's fed on fighting and making up, rescues and escapes. It's a texture on your tongue like a perfectly crisp apple calling every sense to be present. Its arrival is welcome, rather than awkward or demanding to be filled. There's simply nothing that can be said. The intimacy of the moment tethers you together. It simply *is*. It was a silence Zara and Sofi were quietly proud to have cultivated.

After a few minutes filled only with the hushed clanking of cans in pockets, the graveyard of forgotten houses gave way to a yellowed, overgrown soccer field bordering a three-story brick building. It loomed over the field like a bouncer with missing teeth and a heart tattoo, daring anyone to set foot there that didn't belong. Only the lonely remaining letters *SC - - OL* plastered above the rusted double doors hinted that it used to be a lively hub of education.

Runaway Heights. The Heights. Home.

"Home sweet home," Sofi said, as she sighed happily at the monstrosity. "Always looks beautiful after a narrow escape."

Zara nodded. It might be ugly, dirty, crumbling, drafty, and filled with a dozen other street kids who thought she was a freak, but it was home. More than any other place she'd lived in the last six years, anyway.

"Let's head on in." She jiggled the swollen front pocket of her hoodie. "I'm sure Eric is anxious to see us home safe."

"Wouldn't want to keep the boss waiting, now, would we?" Sofi said mischievously. The implied *nudge-nudge-wink-wink* telegraphed between them, and Sofi waggled her eyebrows.

Zara rolled her eyes dramatically. "Oh my god, Sofi, shut up."

She tried to sound serious, but a tiny sliver of amusement leaked through – the fuzzy chemical remnants of their successful lift and serene walk home still had her, if just barely. The situation with Eric wasn't new or particularly funny to her, but it was never far from the surface. Sofi liked to tease her, but Zara tried not to snap at her friend about it, even if it did slice at her heart every time.

"Fine, you old curmudgeon," Sofi said. She made an over-exaggerated bow towards the break in the property's hedges. "Ladies first."

As Zara picked a careful path across the neglected soccer pitch, Sofi stood casually near a tree on lookout duty, pretending to bop along to music through headphones that weren't attached to anything. This abandoned school, loving called "Runaway Heights" or "The Heights" by its residents, was one of the city's best-kept underground secrets, and it had to stay that way. When you're sheltering runaway teens, there's always someone sniffing around looking to cash in on reward money and truancy citations. Secret passageways, irregular entrance protocol, and simple vigilance, supplemented by the crudest of security tech, helped prevent an all-out routing of the building's population. Residents had to enter one at a time, unobserved; keeping your mouth closed if the fuzz interrogated you was one thing, but getting across the lawn without being spotted was another.

  Zara made a beeline for the discolored brick on the east side of the building, carefully scanning the perimeter for potential threats as she went. Dealers, hobos, and bimbos weren't a big deal – they minded their own business - but every once in a while a jogger in a grey sweatsuit would turn up with his German shepherd and make several laps around the school. No sign of Not-A-Cop-at-All today, though.

  Zara slipped through the heavy side door and gave Sofi the high sign.

They popped into the building on the far side of the cafeteria, one of a scant handful of habitable rooms in the old schoolhouse. By unspoken consensus, and long before Sofi and Zara's time, only a quarter of the Heights' potential living space had residents: a smattering of classrooms converted into bedrooms, the cafeteria serving as both dining hall and common room, the art room a makeshift workshop. Nothing more than absolutely necessary. The nature of teenagers is to hold themselves warily apart, but once out of the nest and into the world, it seemed safer to keep within arm's reach of one another. Plus, it made it easier to clean the place.

Four or five late-lunching heads turned as Zara and Sofi walked across the cracked tile floor and headed for the pantry. Sitting in an empty row of peg seats at one table, two nervous-looking boys wolfed down today's watery chili after returning from their own run – their first as newbie residents. Not far away, a clutch of older kids were engrossed in a card game, but they perked up as Sofi passed, giving her a thumbs-up and hooting for her to join them. Sofi waved, calling out names and grinning at the attention, saying she'd be right back. But Zara kept her eyes glued to the ground, intent on making her way to the next door as quickly as possible, the adrenaline fuzzies worn off and her face unreadable.

That still confounded Sofi. She knew, but hated to accept, that all the warmth and enthusiasm her friend had while out on a run was only a temporary high. But unless her brain was awash in hormonal intoxicants, Zara was a million miles away, tucked inside herself. Sofi tried not to let it get to her; the evasive, vague stories about her past that Zara had shared were unspeakably tragic, true, but Sofi struggled to understand how nothing could get through to that armored heart. She just couldn't fathom how someone could be so shut down and afraid of other people.

Especially when there was someone like Eric right in front of you.

The officially unofficial mayor Runaway Heights could always be found bustling around the place with his hands in a project, his mop of thin, white-blonde hair hanging in his eyes as he fixed the generator, charmed new arrivals, or tracked the group's resources on his laptop, which he swears fell off the back of a truck. His high-beam smile radiated a gentle, attentive energy, and he was never too tired to help. Not even after the massive storm last winter when he shoveled a literal ton of snow, repaired every broken window and door, and didn't sleep until everyone was accounted for, warm in their beds. Rumor around the place had it he was powered by snack cakes and Mountain Dew.

Even though Eric was a few years older than most of the residents, practically ancient at 22, it only seemed to endear him to everyone. Having a worldly guy around made everyone feel safer, like someone was watching out for them. His laid-back attitude and drama-handling skills smoothed ruffled feathers and turned the Heights into a haven instead of a teenage-hormone battleground. He'd made the place work in his four years here, the longest anyone had ever stayed, and that earned him hefty doses of respect, as well as a pretty collection of admirers.

But he only had eyes for one person.

Eric turned at the sound of the door, flashing his bright-white smile at Zara. "Hey!" he said, setting aside the laptop and standing to greet them. He cast a calculating glance over both of their lumpy sweaters. "Looks like you did alright out there. What'd you bring me?"

Zara looked up but quickly flicked her gaze past him as she made her way to the shelves and out of the line of conversational fire. It wasn't that she didn't want to talk to him; she just... didn't want to talk to him. She'd had a pretty good day so far, and it'd be a shame to ruin it with all that awkwardness. Better stick to the job and avoid tripping over herself back into that particular quagmire.

Eric looked after her as she passed, face falling briefly before Sofi stepped up to fill the gap. She couldn't stand that puppy-dog look.

"We got it all this time," she said as she started emptying sleeves and pockets into a dump bin. "I don't think we can hit this place again for a while, though." She rolled her eyes and told him the story.

"No worries," he said kindly. "Plenty of other places that haven't seen you in a while, plus it could be time to take another shot at that upscale grocery by the interstate. You guys are probably getting tired of the same old dives, anyway."

He stepped back slightly, trying to include Zara in the conversation. "What do you think, Z? Ready to make Heights history?"

Zara offered only an incoherent noise in response and didn't turn around. She'd already started shelving her loot and seemed absorbed in the work. It was almost obsessive the way she organized the food, making sure each label lined up perfectly and moving the oldest stuff up front. The entire pantry looked as if an artist had stocked it. And technically, one had. When Zara wasn't painting, drawing, or collaging, she was in the storage room, making a meticulous mosaic of dry goods. It was her favorite chore; arranging the brightly-colored packages soothed her jangled nerves and gave her an outlet for leftover creative juices.

Eric waited for her to answer a few seconds longer than necessary. He knew better than to think she'd respond, but he always hoped.

But she just kept stocking, turning cans by millimeters until they were just right. Eric sighed softly and shook his head. With a resigned shrug at Sofi, he picked up the laptop and got back to updating the Excel sheets.

The room filled with the buzzing of the computer and the scooting of canned goods on the wooden shelves. Sofi looked from Zara to Eric and back again from the middle of the awkwardly-quiet room. It'd been a year since "The Incident," but the two still hadn't figured out how to live in the same space without friction. He kept trying his hand, ranging from neutral buddy to keen suitor; she kept accidentally encouraging him or flat-out rejecting his advances. Leaving Sofi to play referee.

But after the excitement of the afternoon's run and the warm welcome in the cafeteria, she wasn't in the mood to call penalties on the game. Exasperation set in. She huffed her annoyance, muttered a word of excuse, and swept out of the storage room back to the cafeteria, leaving the not-a-couple alone.

Let them sort it out today – I've got a poker game to win.

Zara artfully tweaked the aesthetic of the pantry after everything had been put away. Eric tabulated food incomes and projections on the laptop.

Minutes oozed between them, thick with that "I'm so not paying attention to you, but I really am" vibration. Every so often one of them would peek over their shoulder to see if the other was looking. They weren't. At least, not just then.

Eventually, Eric finished his tabulations and clicked the computer shut. Rubbing his screen-tired eyes and unable to delay his departure any longer, he decided to play his ace.

"Hey Z," he said, standing up and stretching. "Dave came back from his run with a box of pastels he picked up on accident. He was going to throw them out, but I convinced him they'd be worth trading." He took a couple of long-legged strides over to her side of the room. "I can have 'em to you by dinnertime, if you want."

Zara's posture shifted slightly. Art supplies were hard to come by in the Heights, and they were a sure-fire way to get her attention. Give her some spraypaint or posterboard, and she'd light up like Christmas. It was like talking to a completely different person – the dark waif would evaporate and this holy virtuoso appeared in her place. Pencil, crayon, paint, paper, canvas, overpass - it didn't matter. All that was important was getting the art out. The promise of new supplies should've caused at least a muted squee. But she didn't even turn around.

Maintain... No good going all soft for fancy crayons.

She tried to telepathically suggest that he fuck off and leave her alone.

Rather of fucking off, though, he leaned on the wall next to her, arms crossed in what he hoped was cool-guy fashion, and tried again. "I know you're running low after that last batch of florals."

In fact, she hadn't had anything to work with at all in weeks. Underneath the ice-queen exterior, Zara was practically leaping at the idea of pastels, but she didn't want Eric to just give them to her. Gifts meant obligation; obligation meant... the sort of situation she wanted to avoid. She didn't want him getting all soppy-romantic and thinking things were any different than she intended.

"Thanks, but I'll get them myself," she said distantly, appearing engrossed in making sure the ramen packets lined up. "I've got a couple bucks and some Twinkies saved up."

Eric's face scrunched in annoyance at the brush-off, but he pushed down the frustration. It was the same every time: flirtation met with a stone-cold shoulder. Discouraging, to say the least. Even he thought that eventually he'd take the hint and pursue an easier target – he certainly had his pick - but he couldn't shake the hum in his heart when he looked at her. Not knowing the firecracker genius she was. Not seeing how her hard edges fit his own. Not after everything that happened last fall.

He sighed softly and ran a hand through his hair, sliding his back down the wall to sit heavily on a milk crate. Surprised at the show of defeat, Zara finally turned to face him. All the lights had gone out in his face, and he stared at a spot on the floor; he suddenly looked older and more exhausted than he'd ever let on. Maybe she'd pushed too far.

Or just far enough.

"What?" she said, a little more harshly than she'd meant to.

He paused before answering, trying to find the exact right words to say a novel's worth of emotion. Eventually, he whispered, "Why do we dance around like this, Zara? I thought you felt the same way I do, but you push back so hard. After the gazebo…"

Zara blushed hard as the memory of cool grass and slick sweat jumped into her mind, filling her up with remnants of sticky emotional fluff and sensuous urgency. The phantom whisper of sincere promises and sweet adoration echoed in her ears, calling up the hazy pinky-purple glow of being held so perfectly safe that not even time could find you. She could even smell a wisp of lake water mixed with manly soap.

Everything softened as her eyes found his for the first time in weeks, maybe months. There, she could see the daily hurt she'd poured into him, all the desperate wounds she'd inflicted in trying drive him away. To protect him. To protect herself. In that moment, she wanted to take it all back. Tell him she was sorry. Wrap him in her arms and swear a thousand times that she would never do it again. That she was his and he was hers and that's how it would always be.

But a tiny voice cut through the cotton-candy dream.

Remember the last time? Remember every *time?*

Her blush turned instantly into anger that singed her cheeks for being weak enough to think about it again, even for a second. Shame rose in her throat and turned her tongue to acid.

"You just don't get it, do you, Eric?" she spat, voice low. She took a step back and crossed her arms protectively over her chest. "It's not like that, it wasn't like that, and it'll never be like that."

The confident voice cracked slightly, but she plunged on, fueled by a mix of hot desire and cold rage. "Find someone else to fall in love with."

She was out the door before he could retort, the ultimatum so sharp he didn't know he'd been cut until it was too late to recover.

Zara fled through the echoing hallways, eyes barely open and holding back frustrated tears, picking her way by memory from storage to her bedroom on the second floor as her mind raced.

The door was open, so she barreled right in, flopping down on her all-black bed before she even registered that Sofi was there. Sometimes having a roommate sucked; you couldn't have a nervous breakdown without being watched.

Sofi sat cross-legged on her own bed at the other side of the room without saying anything. She pretended to be freshly fascinated by Zara's furry animal paintings and flower drawings plastered all over the dingy walls; she also pretended to have not been scribbling furiously in her diary, stuffing the battered notebook under her pillow. The only other time she'd seen Zara in meltdown mode, it'd been after she narrowly avoided a truant officer trying to haul her back to child services. Getting hysterics out of such a stony girl required nothing short of catastrophe.

To her credit, Sofi waited a full five minutes before curiosity overwhelmed her.

"What happened, Z?"

Zara had buried her face in her pillow and didn't respond.

"Was it Eric?"

"..."

"C'mon, you can tell me," Sofi wheedled. "Ooh! Did you guys make out? If you did, I promise I won't tell anybody."

A low warning growl came from Zara's pillow.

Sofi huffed overdramatically. "Fine, be that way. What good is it being heterolifemates if we can't talk about boys?"

She pulled her diary out and started writing again, pretending to ignore Zara's hissy fit. She'd come around eventually. Well, she usually did. But sometimes all those emotions got swallowed, like blood from a broken nose

An impressive stretch of nothing spooled out into the tiny room, filling up the corners. It lapped over the threadbare carpet and seeped onto the bare concrete, washing up where baseboards should've been. A mountain of laundry shed a few articles out of embarrassment. Unspoken words hung heavy off the stacks and piles of artwork, practically dripping with the need to be said. It was a demanding silence made of fear and urgent waiting - the polar opposite of the perfect silence of their walk home that afternoon.

Sofi didn't do well with the cold shoulder; she had never been the patient sort. She snapped her diary shut after a few drawn-out minutes, bounced off her crazy-quilt, and plopped down on the other bed. She craned her face down to the pillow under which her friend had buried herself to make sure Zara heard her.

"I know you won't answer, but let me tell you what I know," she said with the airy tone of someone trying to make light of a serious situation. "Blind monkeys could tell Eric's in love with you, what with all the stupid jokes and little presents and whatnot. And deep down in that cold, black heart of yours, I know you at least like him back. You fight too hard for it to be anything else."

She paused.

"Plus, rumors get around here pretty damn fast. Everybody's known about you guys hooking up for so long it's not even exciting anymore."

A mortified rumble from the pillow.

Sofi grinned a little to herself. If it'd been her in that gazebo, she sure as hell wouldn't be angsting about it like this. The way she heard it, those exploits were something to be damn proud of. But not for Zara.

"What I don't know," she continued, "is why you can't just hook up with Eric for real, not this one-night stand bullshit. It all seems kind of pointless to keep pushing him away when you obviously want him."

Thankfully, Zara rolled over instead of letting the awkwardness get worse. Her face was pink, but there were no tears in her eyes, and her thin jaw had clenched like a fist.

"You know why," she said, her voice sharp and cold between her teeth. "You know better than anyone else."

She did.

Sofi sat up and pulled her legs onto the thin mattress, looking like a petite blonde Buddha. "I know, sweetie. But it's so hard for me to wrap my brain around it. You've been free for so long - aren't you tired of fighting to keep people away? Don't you want to melt a bit?"

Zara bit her lip, her face flickering with the struggle of what to say. She hated these conversations.

But Sofi had a point. She couldn't keep brushing Eric off, hoping her borderline cruelty would eventually scare him away. Apart from everything else, it made her feel like a huge bitch. In the deepest, most remote corner of her heart, though, she knew he was just a catalyst, forcing her to confront demons, tempting her with the promise of something real. The shadows she'd been offered and fallen for in her past life had sewn her up as tightly as the seams of a life preserver. It would need more than a pretty face, kind words, and a flicker-frame movie moment to tear out those stitches.

And yet...

Zara sighed heavily, shaking her head clear and closing her eyes tight as if that would protect her from her own vulnerability.

"I do want to melt. I want it so fucking bad, Sofi," she whispered. "As jealous as people are about Eric chasing me, I'm a zillion times more jealous that you can be happy. I watch you go through life feeling everything, not just the gross shit and adrenaline highs I'm stuck with. But you're the only person I've been able to get close to in years - everybody else tried to throw me away like human garbage. It's made my whole world all washed out and ugly and suspicious because I can't remember what it's like to *not* be this way."

She flinched when Sofi squeezed her leg. She knew her friend was trying to reassure her that she was listening, but Zara was so unused to the sensation of someone else's touch that it nearly hurt.

Zara exhaled slowly, as if the weight of her confession had winded her. Opening her eyes, her gaze fell on a huge canvas hung directly over her bed. The entire ceiling was covered in a tangle of roses all in carmine, claret, and crimson, held together with jagged black stems. It had taken her nearly a week to complete, scavenging and stealing more and more acrylic paint from the art store, painstakingly filling in shadows and light, refusing to sleep until it was finished.

"Mom grew roses," she said, her voice suddenly dreamy and far away. "Huge, blood-red things. Bushes covered the entire backyard. She won awards every year. I never understood it as a kid – how she could spend hours, in all kinds of weather, pruning and feeding those stupid flowers.

"One day, after she grounded me for hiding a bombed report card, I ran out to the garden and beat the shit out of her favorite rosebush. Just wailed on it with a stick until it was trashed." A crooked smile. "Figured that'd show her who was boss.

"But when it was all done, I freaked. I burst out sobbing right there in the dirt. Not only did I absolutely know I'd get my butt whooped, but I knew I'd done something awful.

"Mom came home from work as I was propping up the busted stems, trying to make it look okay. She immediately figured out what had happened, of course. She crossed the yard so fast, getting ready to bawl me out. But I guess she saw all my fear when I looked up and flinched, ready for a swat, because instead she sat down on the ground next to me.

"When I stopped crying and blubbering apologies all over the place, she reached out and gathered me up into her lap. She said, 'Zara, do you know why I care about these roses so much?' I just shook my head. And she said, 'Because they're a perfect expression of love. They're soft and beautiful on the outside, but they're strong and busy inside. They turn the nothing of sun and air into something real that gives us joy just by looking at it. Roses, my sweet little girl, are a beautiful mess of life that deserves to be carefully cared for, just like you.'

"And then she booped me on the nose and hugged me tight and sent me back in the house while she started uprooting and burying the bush I'd destroyed."

Zara tapered off as she choked on the last few words, fighting tears. A few gulps of air steadied her enough to finish the story.

"That's what I want," she said, pointing to the vast floral painting above her. "I want to feel like I've got roses bursting out of my chest, rooted right down in my heart and swallowing up rain and sun and air to turn into real happiness. A beautiful mess of life, right here inside me."

They don't tell you how it's going to be when you get there. They want you to go expecting the very best - pancake breakfasts and trips to the zoo with adoring grownups who buy you everything you ask for. Sure, there are whispers from old hands, the ones who were passed over and are rotting in the guts of the system. They say it with their eyes, too afraid to open their cracked mouths. "Run away," they beg you. "You will die here." But you don't believe it - not at first.

You want to think that you're special, different, unique, just like your dead mommy always told you you were. That you're immune to the disintegration of spirit and degradation of self that's poisoned every child before you. That it won't happen to you because you're perfect.

But it does happen to you. It happens to all of us.

They smile and nod sympathetically when the soft-hearted social worker drops you off in the strangers' doily-and-landscape-oil-paintings living room. They offer you cookies and milk. Show you your new room. Introduce you to your new siblings, your new dog, your new fish. The too-big dress they bought you as a welcome gift. They laugh nervously and say you'll grow into it, knowing the promise they're making. You don't laugh when they say they'd like it very much if you would call them Mom and Dad. They do take you to the zoo, though, to the movies, to restaurants you never dreamed existed.

They adore you because they feel sorry for you.

And the instant you don't reciprocate, the moment you refuse to come out of the rose-pink room because you can't bear to see the light of another day where you are alone with strangers and afraid of living... Fretful phone calls to head office. Google searches for "troubled teen therapists."

Or.

The friendly social worker's van pulls away and suddenly it's time for bed at 3pm. There is no new room or pretty dress or trip to the zoo. There's only knuckle-abrading chores and a barely-clean corner of the basement. There's only a pair of leathered hands in the dark, touching secret places. You pray every day and every afternoon and every night for someone to hear your telepathic pleas for intervention.

Eventually, someone with densely-written papers and a pair of handcuffs does come. But they always come too late.

And then.

Back into the hopper with another set of strangers who only see a sad orphan girl who's been prescribed three anti-psychotics and draws freakishly well on anything you give her and is not a real person because how could she be with so many years of foster care under her belt?

Time after time, home after home, you pry open your heart, choosing again and again through sheer hard-headedness to dare hope this mom will understand, this dad will keep his hands to himself, these strangers can be a family. That someone will keep you close to their heart without abandoning you in a matter of months. Or will know you are your own property, not theirs.

It happens to all of us.

It happened to me.

All I have ever wanted, since I was ten years old and couldn't want easy things anymore, like a pony or to go to Disneyland with my (dead) mom and (dead) dad and (dead) brother, is for someone to see me for who I am and to love me without having to pay for it with my tears or my sweat or my body. To not be eviscerated when I inch open the lead-lined doors sealing up my heart. To be happy without being tainted by the fear of "how long?" To have a Technicolor roller coaster of emotions instead of this broken grey carousel of anger and guilt and shame.

To be a real girl.

"I know you're in there, Snake! Come out or I'll have the SWAT team up your ass so fast your next thought will be wrapped around a barrel."

An AK slid across the floor to Fox's feet.

"Smart move. Maybe if you'd been that smart two days ago, I wouldn't be here."

Snake walked out, hands upraised. Fox took one hand off his sidearm and opened the radio channel. "Alright, boys, take him down."

"The fuck, man?! You said -- "

"I know what I said, you dumb shit. Think I'm going to bargain with every Russian-armed felon I meet?"

The FBI agent grinned as four SWAT uniforms descended on Snake.

"Um, excuse me, miss?"

Zara looked up sharply from her book. Trashy crime novels were her favorite way to pass the time when she sold her excess paintings, but she tended to get so absorbed in the drama that she missed a few sales.

"Yeah?"

The woman standing in front of her was clearly not from this part of town. Nobody down here wore a designer trenchcoat, much less those huge bug-eye shades. Most of the city was filled with the sort of human detritus folks of a certain income level – folks like this lady - like to pretend don't exist. It makes them feel guilty to think of all those teen runaways, destitute families, and jobless grunts. Instead, they perch safely ensconced in their million-dollar homes on the edge of town, looking down on the smog-stained masses. When they did venture into the prole habitat to slum it up in the greasy clubs, you could pick them out in seconds. But, fortunately for Zara and the handful of other street-vending artists, the townies always had plenty of money to burn, and this one was no exception.

"I was wondering who the artist is," Designer Lady said, gesturing to the dozen or so canvases behind Zara. "I'm a bit of a collector of woodland artwork, and I'm just dying to have those delightful deer pieces. They're so lifelike and moving – perfect for my husband's den."

A collector of woodland artwork? What does that even mean?

Rather than get too snarky, Zara simply said, "The artist? That would be me."

"You? Really?" She looked slightly aghast.

"Really, really."

Designer Lady looked from Zara to the paintings and back again a couple of times like a cartoon character. Zara had been selling her work for about a year, but it still seemed like anyone over 25 was totally unwilling to believe that a dirty street kid could be responsible for artwork so beautiful. Even in elementary school, she'd been brilliant with a brush, creating fully-formed people when most kids were still struggling with stick figures. It all came so easily. Caring art teachers had guided her talent with after-school mentoring, revealing a whole new mode of expression in her otherwise dark little world. She'd even had one particularly lifelike cat portrait hung in a local gallery before dropping out. But here on the street, it strained most people's credulity to equate her creative skill with her ruffian look.

"Are you going to buy anything or not?" Zara huffed, after a short minute, waving her book a bit for emphasis. "I'm kinda busy here."

"What? Oh! Yes, yes, of course," the woman stammered. "How much for that big one with the stag and doe?"

"Usually, those go for three or four hundred. But I'll give it to you for two." Zara flashed her best reeling-in-a-customer smile. She'd sold better paintings for less, but she wanted to get back to her book.

"Fantastic!" Designer Lady exclaimed.

To Zara's surprise, she reached in her purse and pulled out a fat wad of twenties. She gingerly tossed ten of them into the empty coffee can at Zara's feet, as if coming too close might catch her something contagious, then she was down the street, clicking the trunk button on her oversized van and zipping away.

"Damn, girl, you totally fleeced that townie, didn't you?"

Sofi came ambling along the sidewalk behind Zara, hands in her jeans pockets and a folded camp chair slung over her shoulder. She usually showed up to these vendor jaunts, more for security than conversation – this was an up-and-coming area, but it hadn't quite gotten there yet. A girl couldn't be too sure what might happen. Not that Sofi would actually be much protection – she was really only dangerous to intruding flies in the summer – but it was comforting to have her around.

Zara smiled at her friend and put the book down. "Totally. I won't lie – I kinda love it when the bubbleheads drop in. They're *so* easy."

"You're awful," Sofi grinned. She dropped her chair and pried it open, the rusty hinges complaining as she sat.

Their familiar silence settled around them as they people-watched from the sidewalk. They could always count on the flow of traffic in and out of the inkshop across the street to entertain them while they waited for another self-proclaimed connoisseur to show up.

Artists at this place had a flair for the dramatic, and their clientele was demanding. It was nothing to see someone walk out sporting a disgustingly lifelike exposed ribcage or a killer whale about to breach. Once, they'd seen a guy come out with his face done up in lizard scales, each one catching the sunlight individually. Tattooing tech had come a long way in the last few years, making modern designs more amazing in general, but these guys obviously had something special. Dozens of shops had gone out of business as this one rapidly stole all their clients. When you're the best, you're the best, no argument.

It always made Zara slightly jealous, though, to see the inkslingers' handiwork so thoroughly enjoyed by both customers and artists alike. She never got that satisfaction from her own work. Canvases and cardboard felt too transient, too easily destroyed or forgotten about; tattoos were forever. Anything that artist put into your skin was burned there for you to see every day until it rotted off your bones. You had no choice but to live with it. Powerful shit.

A sudden movement in the shop's alley caught Zara's eye and derailed her train of thought. Somebody in a white shirt and jeans was waving at her from in front of the dumpster, but across the four-lane road, she couldn't quite make them out.

Artist? Too skinny and not enough tats.

Client? Too ragged-looking.

Hobo? Not ragged enough.

In the middle of her debate, the figure started to cross the four-lane intersection, looking around furtively for speeding cars. Zara nudged Sofi and pointed. They squinted at the stranger, but by the time they reached a verdict, he was already on them.

"Ladies!" Eric chirped. "You'll never guess what I just found." He was grinning so hard Zara was afraid the top of his head might come off.

Sofi perked up. "Ooh, what'd you find?"

"It's a surprise!" he grinned, tucking a battered plastic bag protectively behind his back.

"Eee!" Sofi clapped her hands and bounced like a five-year old at a birthday party. She knew the present wouldn't be for her, but she was one of those crazy people who love surprises. "Is it animal, vegetable, or mineral?" she asked.

"*Errrrt*! None of the above. Have to follow me home and find out," he taunted, chancing a look at Zara, whose smile evaporated.

He dropped his voice conspiratorially and glanced around in a way best described as "checking for the feds." He said, "Can't talk about it here. Someone might be listening, you know."

The girls rolled their eyes in tandem. Eric could be such an unabashed conspiracy nut. If there was the remotest possibility that The Man had even contemplated the idea of having a hand in something, Eric believed it. Buying a jar of alien slime (that turned out to be shaving gel) from a guy in a back alley bar was just the most recent example.

Too many X-Files reruns, Zara thought, completely circumventing the fact he'd hooked her on the crime novels she couldn't put down.

"Fine," she said in a mock huff. She was feeling sassy after making bank off that idiot deer-lover. "If you're so worried about the government reading your mind, we'll pack up in a bit and meet you at home. That'll give you time to put on your tinfoil hat." She flashed him a smile that she immediately regretted. *Wrong idea.*

"Sweet!" he said. "Maybe I'll make one for you, too, Z." He winked at her, then scampered off towards the Heights.

An hour and change later, though, Eric had to admit he was stumped. When he'd pulled the inkpen from the dumpster and held it up to the light, he could clearly see the problem: under the battered casing, shorted circuitry had blown the power source. Easy enough to fix for someone who'd spent four years in vocational tech and two in a luxury garage.

The stainless steel barrel had been a snap - a buff here, a few taps with a hammer there, and it looked brand-new. The microscopic cluster of high-speed, ultrafine needles just needed a quick round in the old art room's kiln for sterilization. The burnt-out copper wiring had to be replaced, but harvesting trashed computers made that an easy fix. The ink cartridges hadn't been damaged, thankfully; the tiny vials of hyper-last color were the only thing beyond his talents and would've cost hundreds to replace. When he eventually came up for air, face smeared with grease and a few extra volts in his bloodstream, the device was perfect in every way.

Except that it didn't work.

The voltmeter showed electricity flowing through the wires, but flicking the switch did nothing. He even tried hooking it up to a car battery for extra juice. On, off, on, off, on, off. Plugged in, unplugged. Cuss it, beg it. Zero.

Fuck.

Defeated, Eric flumped onto the workbench and fumed for a bit in the sawdust. He'd repaired everything from cars to watches, tweaking the insides as if he could hear their little voices telling him exactly where it hurt. One brutal summer, when the Heights' leech connector to the power grid went down, he'd built a generator from scrap and duct tape to run fans until he could repair the cable. He'd be damned if a six-inch bundle of wires would beat him – he had a reputation to uphold.

And don't forget about her.

The thought landed like a hot ice cube down his shirt, producing both warm fuzzies and the willies. He picked up the lifeless inkpen with two fingers and looked at his reflection in its surface, checking to see if he had "sucker" branded on his forehead. Or "obsessive romantic." Or maybe "stalker." Some days, it sure felt like it.

He certainly didn't mean to come off like a creeper. All he'd ever wanted from Zara was a chance, cliché as it was, just one shot to reach out and show her he actually cared. The intensity in her artwork, the way she seemed to barely touch the world, the conflicted need to burst herself open – more than the way she looked, those things fueled his affection. The hint of a powerful soul just under the skin kept drawing him in, no matter how cruelly she rebuffed him. And friendship had been an uneasy compromise because of it. It'd be easier to know how to act if he had a clear signal from her, some undisputable line in the sand saying that night in the gazebo was only a momentary fling. But the not-quite-accidental brushes while they stocked the pantry, the warm smiles when he made a joke, and the hesitation when he pressed his case – it made the line blurry at best. All the nerves in his body twanged like an oceanside dowsing rod knowing she wanted to reach out and take his hand. Even if it made him look a little stalkery, he couldn't risk ignoring that evidence and losing her altogether.

Patience.

He sighed. Picking up the inkpen as a gift for Zara had seemed like an awesome idea at the time; now it seemed like another bullet point on an eventual restraining order.

He was halfway to the trashcan with it when the door popped open and the girls strolled in, their hair damp from the showers. The smell of tangerine shampoo cut through the workshop's acrid metal and oil reek like an incredibly girly invasion as they crossed to the bench where Eric stood frozen in mid-toss. He pulled his hand back in a not terribly smooth recovery and laid the inkpen on the table next to him.

Too late now.

"Hey, ladies!" he chimed. "Check it." He gestured grandly at the instrument like a gameshow bimbo displaying a brand new car.

Zara kept her eyes down and pretended to be more interested in a rack of industrial glue than Eric, but Sofi lit up when she spotted the device. She rushed over and held it aloft.

"Holy shit!" she breathed. "Z, look!"

With a petulant huff, Zara obligingly lifted her eyes. A reverse eclipse of sheer delight slid across her face. With a squee of abandon, she sprung forward, barely crossing the intervening distance in her excitement, and snatched the inkpen from Sofi.

The cool metal of the barrel slid like quicksilver through her eager fingers as she rolled it in her hands.

All this time of lusting after the inkslingers' trade and she finally had a pen in her hot little paws. A whole new art form waited in the little casing – something more permanent and more real than anything she'd done before. She couldn't wait to use it.

Glee drenched her brain, and she giggled as she bounced around wildly, like a brainiac getting a full ride to Harvard. She peeled out in unselfconscious laughter, grinning to show all her teeth. She spun around and leapt into Eric's arms, squeezing out all her thanks and happies in a bear hug as strong as her thin frame could manage.

Wait a minute.

Zara froze.

Eric's eyes bulged.

Sofi held her breath.

The sound of gates slamming in Zara's heart was practically audible in the silence, the aftershocks making her tremble. Geologically slowly, she unwound herself from around Eric's chest, feeling the inviting heat of him dissipate from her cheeks as she backed away. One step. Two steps. Three. Bump into the workbench.

Silence. Awkward, statically-charged silence.

Sofi was the first to recover.

"So, uh, you found this in the dumpster?" she asked Eric, pointedly ignoring Zara as the other girl retreated and heaved enormous panic-stricken breaths to calm herself.

But he was staring at Zara, brow furrowed and mouth open in a confused mix of curiosity and alarm. Sofi had to repeat her question a couple of times and snap her fingers in his face before he would stammer an answer.

"Hrm? Oh, yeah. Dumpster."

She waited.

He shook himself and refocused on Sofi. "It was pretty beat up but still salvageable. Good news is it's in perfect shape now. Bad news is I have no idea why it doesn't work."

"And how exactly does that equal perfect shape?"

"Well, it looks right, you know? It's charging, and all the pieces are in place, but it won't power up."

Sofi snorted. "Some mechanic."

As they groused at each other, Zara looked down at the inkpen still clenched in her white-knuckled grip. That couldn't be right. It definitely worked; she could feel the electricity. Looking down, though, the short power cord was forlornly dangling at her waist, several feet from the nearest outlet. Curiosity overcame the hug-nausea.

She flicked the power switch to "on."

A soft buzzing vibrated her hand. The sound layered over itself, overcoming the drone of the workshop's passive appliances, and stealthily filled the room.

"What the fuck's that noise?" Eric said, turning to see if one of the computers had suddenly decided to commit suicide.

Zara held up the purring device as a tiny droplet of red ink plopped onto the concrete floor.

"Works."

A few crowded moments later, the three of them were huddled around the flimsy folding table in the center of the girls' bedroom. Eric had been given special dispensation to come in since he'd been the one to find the inkpen. Besides, they hadn't been able to shut him up after Zara turned it on; he was in full-blown mythbuster mode.

"Maybe it's, like, arc electricity? You weren't too far from an outlet – could've been enough charge in the air."

Sofi shook her head, "You couldn't even get it to work when it *was* plugged in. That doesn't make sense."

"What if it had a loose wire that got knocked into place while Z was jumping around?"

"Still didn't have a power source."

"Alien technology?"

Sarcastic stare.

"Okay, maybe not."

Zara didn't offer any solutions. She simply sat in her creaky folding chair and switched the inkpen on and off, the cord draped uselessly over the tabletop. Energy surged up and down her arm, tickling the nerves and skin with the same bubbly sensation she associated with petty larceny, making her brain fizz pink and purple. Layers of strange joy laid themselves down over her heart and trickled out of the corners of her mouth as they twitched a smile. She could feel the power ebb and flow with every flick of the switch, tugging the emotional sugar rush back and forth. Turning it on felt like her arm was complete after years of having no hand; turning it off felt like losing it all over again.

And under the roar of remembering long-forgotten pleasure, a voice, both familiar and totally foreign, pinged in the recesses of her mind. Stainless steel and color swirling to form itself into impressions of words and meaning.

Click.

"It's a circuit," she whispered.

Sofi and Eric stopped their bickering and looked at her quizzically.

"It needs me," she continued. "Maybe that's why the inkslingers threw it out and you couldn't get it to work. Nobody had the right connection to power it." She looked at the limp cord, then up at her friends. "But I do. It's getting it whatever it needs directly from me, like a battery."

Sofi raised an incredulous eyebrow and opened her mouth to scoff, but Eric's face opened wide with understanding and he cut her off.

"Like... magic?"

Zara looked like she'd rather swallow a bowl of carpet tacks than agree, but there wasn't another answer. She nodded.

"Oh, snap!" Eric whooped. "You have no idea how long I've been tracking stuff like this! There's this whole underground supernatural population that the government's busting because they don't want 'normal people' to believe in it. Bad for control." He rubbed his hands together eagerly. "I can't believe you're one of them, Z!"

She laughed in spite of herself.

"How cool is that?! Come on, let's test it out!" Sofi squeaked.

They looked at each other, suddenly hesitant. Finding out you (or your best friend) might have some kind of mystical mojo is one thing – testing it out is quite another.

After a few seconds of nervous contemplation, Eric pointed at Sofi. "You should go first."

Made sense. She'd been going on for months about how badly she wanted to get some ink done but could never put together the cash. More important things, like eating, tended to come up too often. Zara had teased her for being chicken, but just the suggestion had Sofi quivering with anticipation and put a grin on her face.

"Are you sure you want me to go first?" she asked. Her voice was sharp with excitement, but she was fighting to be calm and polite like her momma had taught her. Old habits die hard.

"Totally," said Zara, smiling warmly at her for the first time in ages. It came surprisingly easily, bright, not forced. It wasn't full-on-floodlights, but she'd be happy with a nightlight for now.

Sofi squeed and flung off her black Misfits hoodie to reveal a threadbare but still bright pink *My Little Pony* tee underneath.

The other two stared.

"What?" she bristled defensively. "I can't like cartoons?"

Zara smirked and Eric stifled a chuckle. Sofi liked to put up a tough-girl front, mostly to keep up with Zara's "I don't give a fuck" coolness. But there was a squishy nougat center of ultra-girliness in there that demanded attention. She'd been caught reading fashion magazines and painting her toenails more than once, the offending spy getting a knuckle sandwich for their pains.

She glared at them, the dare to say something hanging in the air.

"What do you want, Soph?" asked Zara, heading off what could've been an interesting fight. "I don't think you've ever said."

To her surprise, the other girl actually blushed. Sofi looked down at her shoes before answering in the quietly embarrassed tones of a teenager forced to sit on Santa's lap.

"I've always wanted a bear paw print." Foot shuffle. "You know, like a real one walked on me, not that tribal crap. Something realistic." Shuffleshuffle. "But we totally don't have to do it if you think it's stupid."

"Why's that stupid?" asked Eric. "Bears are awesome! They're all *rawr* and eating campers and shit."

He cocked his head and narrowed his eyes at her. "What's it mean, though? Gotta have some personal meaning." He rolled up his sleeve and pointed at the over-embellished script on his forearm reading *G & F'N R*. "Never, ever, ever get a tattoo just 'cause."

Zara chimed in, "Yeah, I refuse to contribute to the stockpile of regrettable tattoos. Ask me for a tramp stamp, and you're banned from this room for life."

Sofi's blush deepened. "It's personal, okay?" she said, voice shifting into borderline-tantrum-toddler in its insistence. "But that's what I want, so that's what I'm asking for. What's with all the freaking questions?!"

Zara held her hands up in a peacemaking gesture. "Okay, okay! Nobody's asking any more questions."

To Eric, she said, "Maybe you should give us some privacy."

He opened his mouth to protest, but the intensity of the stinkeye he got shut him up immediately. Knowing when you're beat is an important life skill, after all. He headed out with his characteristic springy step, and Zara locked the door behind him.

"Now," Zara said as she pushed up her sleeves. "Let's get you tattooed, young lady."

It is ease. Flow. Waves. Undulation.

It rushes. Bounds. Surges. Escapes.

No pattern, no idea of design. Just gogogo. The machine craves, demands, requires my connection, pulls invisible wires in my heart. It reaches into my well and drags up an overflowing bucket of the thirst I so desperately hide, pouring it over my head, making me gasp from the shock. It needs me awake, alive, aroused so it can sculpt the world in flesh, needs my repression, compression, obsession as fuel. We cannot move in tandem if only one of us is working.

I give it power to have power over me. I'm an instrument of an instrument. I am both source and servant.

And for my reward, endlessly exhausting ecstasy. Curves and edges sizzle in my nerve endings as if touching the needle to my own flesh. The rawness caged in the device bursts from me; I'm afraid it will shatter, shredded by the sheer momentum of molecules pounding in my fingertips. Speed and form, beauty and pain, tension and release. It brings me to the brink and back over and over until I can't lay down one more line.

Only then is it finished.

"Oh, Z..." Sofi marveled, admiring the design in the full-length mirror behind their door.

The darkly-shaded bear's paw caressed the soft curve of her upper arm, the size of her own palm, each black claw digging into the top bone of her shoulder. It only took two hours, a combination of Zara's adrenaline and skill, the minimal design, and whatever juju flowed through the inkpen itself. Tinges of burnt orange and dirt brown in layers and edges gave the impression of a heavy footprint just left by a momma bear on the prowl. A photograph in high definition, etched into skin.

"Oh, Z," she repeated. There weren't any other words.

Zara was rooted to her folding chair, inkpen on the table, arms hanging limply, eyes slightly glazed and staring out into space. Exhaustion visibly clung to her like sweat, tangible in the cramped room. It was contagious; looking at Zara about to sway and slump over gave Sofi vertigo. She instantly felt like she was passing-out drunk.

"I think," she slurred, the urge to sleep overtaking her brain, "we need to lie down."

Zara didn't respond, just kept looking dumbly into the distance. Sofi sighed and stuck her hands in Zara's armpits, dragging her fully-clothed into bed. She sagged a bit; a scrawny little twig like Zara shouldn't weigh so damn much. Zara's grateful eyes sparkled as she looked up at her friend, her eyelids drooping into dreamland.

Sofi pulled the covers up and whispered, "Sleep sweet, Z."

She climbed into her own bed carefully, making sure to cover the fresh ink on her shoulder with a scrap of gauze from the first-aid kit in the hallway before pulling the t-shirt back on. Hunkering down into the musty blankets, she let the remaining free-floating nervous energy of the tattoo session dissolve into the sudden fatigue that had engulfed them both. It tucked her in like a mother.

And in that slippery instant between wakefulness and dreaming, she could have sworn she felt the brush of fur against her cheek.

Zara woke up alone.

Sofi's bed was empty but immaculately made, and the whole room had been tidied, including Mount Laundry, which had been folded and stowed. The raucous collection of Zara's paintings on various flat surfaces had been lovingly dusted. Even their unscrupulously-acquired DVD collection had been alphabetized, from *Battlestar Galactica* to *Star Wars*. In her bleary-headed state, Zara wondered if someone had broken into their room – some diabolically OCD maid out to clean all the things.

In all the time Zara and Sofi had been bunking together, their room had never been so clean. Sofi's side of the room was perpetually covered in punk fan paraphernalia and sprinkled with lumps of what Zara could only assume used to be food but were now tiny ecosystems. With only the occasional drying canvas or stray pair of underwear wandering about, Zara's looked positively gleaming by comparison. To see the place suddenly so starkly neat felt weird.

She shrugged and hauled herself out from under the covers, deciding to be grateful for small miracles. Not bothering with shoes or brushing her teeth, she shuffled down the grubby corridor towards the cafeteria. Ostensibly she was looking for Sofi, but really, she needed to eat something and get her bearings. The euphoric aftershocks of the tattoo session had dissipated, leaving her with cottonmouth and a spinning headache, like she'd had an entire bottle of whiskey to herself. In the whole span of her creative life, she'd never been so supremely present for the work and so utterly drained afterwards. Not even the time she tried her hand at metal sculpture and wound up making a complete 1:10 scale stegosaurus out of stainless steel in eight straight hours, all by herself. She grinned at the memory; the art teacher had nearly peed herself with dino-nerd excitement.

She swung open the cafeteria's double doors to find all the residents of Runaway Heights clustered in a tight knot at the center of the room. A dozen young bodies held in tight anticipation, burning with attention. It couldn't be a fight because the entire room was completely silent. Twenty-four eyes were fixated on something in the middle of the mob, but all Zara could hear was someone counting quietly under their breath.

Intrigued, she sidled up beside Eric, who was nearest the door, to peer over his shoulder. The oil-and-soap scent of his skin so close nearly unbalanced her as she stood on tiptoe. *Stop that*, she started to scold herself. But the mental lashing broke off when she saw what everyone was staring at.

Sofi was lying on her back, dirty blond hair swirled out on the floor beneath her, balancing a folded cafeteria table on the soles of her feet. No hands. No supports. No sign of strain. Just holding it there like it was the absolute most natural place for a four hundred-pound piece of school equipment. And she was counting.

49...

50...

51...

"What the *fuck* is going on here?!"

Startled, Sofi's head shot up to see Zara standing there, stunned, hands on her hips, and her mouth a thin line of disapproval like a mother who's just caught their son with porn in the bathroom.

Sofi's legs wobbled.

The table slid.

The crowd gasped as one sideshow-watching organism.

And just as the table tilted past ninety degrees, Sofi shoved its edge with her foot and caught it with both hands, delicately guiding the enormous twelve-man lunch table back to the ground as if it were made of cardboard instead of stainless steel.

The crowd burst into wild applause. Sofi stood up and dusted herself off, glowing with pride as she bowed to her audience. Spectators moved towards her for handshakes and hugs, but Sofi wasn't looking at them.

And then they remembered Zara.

The residents of the Heights had a well-developed sense of smell when it came to trouble. Constantly looking over your shoulder for truant officers and parent-hired detectives helped. And even the newest arrivals had honed in on the scent from Zara. Her depression-fueled rages were legendary. Eric had once heard her verbally peeling the skin off a kid who'd asked why she was so creepy. Another time, she'd thrown a TV out a third-story window; her favorite character biting it on a show had thrown her into a three-day funk. Stories like that got around fast, and newbies learned to steer clear, lest they suffer defenestration, as well.

The signal to leave hit every antenna in the crowd at once. Zara's crossed arms and tapping foot likely had something to do with it. A dozen pairs of feet hastily shuffled out of the cafeteria, everyone suddenly remembering Very Important Chores that needed to be done elsewhere.

Only Eric stayed behind; his skin was practically flame retardant from persistent, voluntary exposure to Zara. Plus, he was dying to find out how Sofi had pulled off the stunt. He wasn't a fool, though, and he gingerly stepped out of punching radius.

Sofi, however, boldly stepped forward as the room emptied. "What's the big deal, Z?" she said, miffed to have lost spotlight.

"What do you mean, 'what's the big deal?'!" Zara said, nearly shouting. This stacked on top of the inkpen-hangover, she was coming unhinged. "You just benched three times your weight in seating, and you've never been able to carry the goddamn laundry basket more than a hundred yards without getting winded! How the fuck did you *do* that?!" Her eyes were wide, but with anger or wonder, even she wasn't entirely sure.

Sofi shrugged. "Dunno, really. I woke up feeling like the universe was holding its breath, waiting for me to do something."

"Is that why our room looks like it was attacked by a meth-addicted Mary Poppins?"

"Yeah!" Sofi laughed. "The place was a wreck, and it was nearly all my mess. You were dead to the world, so I thought I'd clean up a little. Seemed like the right thing to do after you did all this amazing work." She gestured to her exposed shoulder.

Zara noticed for the first time Sofi was showing off her new tattoo with a racerback tank top, despite the autumn chill. The design seemed to be glowing faintly to Zara's eyes. Probably a trick of the light – the building's antiquated fluorescent bulbs were constantly on the fritz.

"After that, I was freaking starving," Sofi continued. "Seriously, I could've eaten an entire cow. And when I got down here for breakfast, one of the tables had busted and some of the little guys were trying to move it out of the way, but it wouldn't budge. Figured I'd try to help, so I walked up and... lifted it."

"It's true, Z," Eric broke in. "Tina, Sammy, and Dave couldn't wrangle it out to the shop door, so they begged Sofi to do it since she's bigger and older. Then she got all pissy like she usually does when you ask her to lift anything heavy," he winced as Sofi made a snotty face at him, "but when she put her hands on it, it came clear up off the ground. Spooked the hell out of all of us. But then the kids started asking her to lift more and more stuff, and it kinda just turned into what you saw. She'd been leg-pressing that table nearly three whole minutes before you broke it up."

Sofi was grinning from ear to ear as Eric described her exploits, stretching and flexing a bit. Muscles stood out from her arms, making smooth, firm curves that Zara could've sworn were soft and squishy only yesterday. And she held herself differently. Usually, Sofi slouched to hide her bigness, like she was trying to flip herself inside out, but now she stood ramrod straight, and the sunny confidence she'd always emanated was subdued somehow. She seemed imposing, in a stately and regal way. A mother bear watching over her cubs.

The penny dropped.

Zara's hand flew to her mouth. "Oh my god, Sofi," she half-whispered. "The tattoo."

"The tattoo?" Eric and Sofi said together, sharing a skeptical look.

"Yes, the fucking tattoo!" she repeated, pointing at her friend's arm. "If the inkpen is magic, why wouldn't the tattoo be magic, too?"

They stared at her blankly.

"You're stronger than at least four guys. You developed some kind of weird nesting instinct," Zara explained, voice getting slightly more hysterical with every sentence. "Can't you see the difference?"

Sofi's hand caressed the already-healed design. It did look as if a fully-grown bear had marked her. She could see the new definition in her muscles; things she knew she logically must possess but had never seen before. And as she looked at Eric and Zara, she realized she didn't see two random people who stumbled into her life; she saw responsibility and protection. Anyone trying to come between her and would have to survive her fury. She felt a growl rise in her throat at the mere thought of it.

With all the clarity of a slap to the face, Sofi knew Zara was right.

"How did you...?" she asked.

Zara wailed, "I don't know! None of this makes any fucking sense." Her face fell rapidly as she tried to find a mental handle for the situation.

"Maybe it was me," Sofi said hurriedly.

"How?"

Sofi chewed her bottom lip a bit as she tried to find the words. It was a nervous habit left over from days of stress ulcers wondering if Momma would find the Eminem albums under her bed. A bloody, cracked mouth only made three days of passive-aggressive punishment worse.

Ladies don't look like that. Ladies don't listen to such awful music. Ladies tell the truth. Ladies don't disappoint their parents.

She sank into an empty stool and gathered herself, knowing how crazy she'd sound but not really caring. Something important had happened, and they needed to understand.

"Bears are all about strength and independence and family. They go for months without food or contact with others and come out in perfect health, ready to take on the world. They wander alone for weeks, then fight to the death when something threatens their family. They topple full-grown trees and peel the roofs off trucks!"

She looked down suddenly, the schoolgirl words reddening her face.

"That's who I want to be, the kind of strength I need. I've always been the pitiful girl the popular crowd let tag along because she made everyone else feel good about themselves. I was safe if I stood by and pretended to laugh as they left threats in my real friends' lockers. No matter how much I loved somebody, I couldn't help them because I'm fat and slow and a chickenshit. I could barely protect myself.

"And going home wasn't any better. All the teasing and torment I missed out on at school got dished up there. My older sister, Lili, was the perfect child – star athlete, modeling gigs, full ride scholarships – and all I could ever be was a freak by comparison. My parents did everything they could to force me into her mold, to 'cure' my tomboy streak and 'correct' my attitude, so they didn't have to be embarrassed.

"Every night, I'd lay in bed and pray for whatever god would listen to fix me so I could be stand up for people I loved. To bring me a real family, not people trying to make me different. But it never worked. Not after years of wishing on falling stars. Not after Momma bought those hypnosis DVDs and Daddy sent me to fat camp and Lili shredded my journals. Not even after I ran away."

She choked back a sob. Long seconds stretched around her as she caught her breath and wiped away a renegade tear.

"With this tattoo, though," she continued, laying a hand gently over her tattoo, "I don't have to worry about that anymore."

Both Zara and Eric were gawking at her like she was some kind of endangered animal stepping out of the bush. She could feel the blush trickling into the tips of her ears. The Heights was a strictly "don't ask, don't tell" organization; no one talked about what they left behind. Too personal. Too painful. The idea that this bouncy little cherub-faced girl had ever been depressed or powerless seemed impossible. Yet the longing and ache in her voice laid it bare, an ugly truth in a beautiful mouth.

Sofi wanted to bolt, get out from under the stare, but couldn't. The rawness of telling her story after all these years had shaken something loose. A piece of cosmic understanding you only get when you're looking the other way.

"But you know what? When I originally wanted this, it was a reminder that I'm not weak and that you can choose your family. I had the desire, the seed of the idea, but whatever you did with the inkpen, Zara, that's what made it real. Something in the tattoo. I can feel it in my skin."

She took a deep, bracing breath and plunged on.

"It's not me – I'm just a sad, chubby girl who wanted to be strong. And I can't believe it's the inkpen – that's just a pretty machine," she said slowly, closing her serious brown eyes so she didn't have to see the bomb hit. "That only leaves one other thing it could be."

Zara eyes darted from Sofi's face to the bear paw, sheer disbelief radiating from her pores.

"I... I did that?"

Pause.

Still standing in the middle of the cafeteria, Zara put her head in her trembling hands and sank slowly to the cold tiles, letting the built-up bizarreness of the last twenty-hours wash over her. Design come to life, a taste of real magic. Bear-paws and family secrets. She couldn't handle any more sideswipes to her world and buckled under the weight.

"What is *wrong* with me?" she murmured through a log-jam of tears.

"Oh, sweetie." Sofi moved to wrap her friend in a gentle hug. "Nothing's wrong with you," she said soothingly. "There's something amazingly, wonderfully, uniquely right."

In another city, in another state, the hushed whir of machinery tiptoed between servers, spooling up one marked "Sector 6." A single red light flicked on in the darkened room, triggering a domino effect of computerized responses. The mainframe sent an email to a top-secret address. The door sputtered slightly as the pressurized lock released. The other servers chirped to confirm their presence, like a classroom roll call. The overhead lights snapped into life one at a time, revealing the voluminous Big Room with its fields of sleek, black CPUs occupying every available surface.

Except one.

Across from the server farm, a single, uncrowded wall displayed a sprawling map of the country - a work of art measured in triple-digit square feet, drawn in such detail that Michelangelo would weep to have not painted it himself. Every rise and shift of the land, every creek running through a backyard, every cluster of woods had been painstakingly drawn out. But its beauty was purely functional – a happy accident born of necessity. For the department to track its quarry, attention to detail was paramount.

Only one thing marred the map's scenic perfection. The enormous panorama was covered in millions of tiny red lights dotting the map like acne on a highschooler, each no more than a speck but part of a virulent plague cast over the land. No matter how glamorous or backwoods, if that clutch of civilization contained at least twenty human souls, it had its own shiny landmark. The instant anything worth investigating cropped up, the light beamed the location; the instant someone took the case, it went dark. Simple - lights are like that.

A tentative knock on the bedroom door insinuated itself into Zara's dream but didn't wake her right away. Knocking sounds are normal when you're playing the sexy concubine in the cowboy space captain's quarters. Besides, it was the first dream she could recall that didn't involve shadowy figures chasing, capturing, or coercing her in the darkness, and she was trying to hang onto it. For all she knew, it would be the last.

But the rapping persisted, and eventually she had to leave the captain with nothing but underpants and a confused look on his face. Shifting a bunch of collage-destined magazines caused a tiny avalanche that revealed a cracked digital clock. *6:39am.* Zara groaned like a wounded wildebeest and threw off the thick blankets. The patch of tatty carpet by her bed did nothing to buffer the dead chill from the concrete underneath, and she winced as her bare feet hit the floor.

"Whoever's out there better be dying," she muttered loudly in the general direction of the insistent *taptaptap*.

She snatched the nearest warm thing from the ever-renewing Mount Laundry - Sofi's ratty turquoise bathrobe - and padded miserably to the door. Visions of a brown coat still dancing in her head made her wish, not for the first time, that she could learn some Chinese curses from TV. She popped the door lock and yanked on the handle, opening her mouth to bawl out the intruder with the English ones she did know.

"What in the name of the holy mother of god and all her wacky nephews do you - "

The tiny person in front of her winced, poised to run like a gazelle spotted by a lioness at the watering hole. Zara, taken slightly aback at the reaction, cut off her invective as she tried to call up the boy's name.

Couldn't be more than fourteen. Enormous black glasses with tape at delicate points. Long pianist's fingers and a misplaced boxer's nose. So thin and short the wind from the door should've blown him over.

The new kid. Dave.

She softened a little, choking up on the bathrobe and attempting to smooth her frazzled black mane with her free hand. The rumors about her temper had eventually trampled their way through her ears – sad fury and violent bluster, not unlike an emo hurricane. And the scene she'd made in the cafeteria had only made things worse. She was impressed this wan-faced kid had summoned the courage to walk down the hall without wetting himself, much less rouse her from a dead sleep.

Dave stood there as she sized him up, unsure how his venture into the lioness' den would end. Zara cleared her throat, shifting her tone from "you'll wish I was never born" to "stern schoolteacher".

"What do you want, Dave? It's ass-o'clock in the morning."

"I, uh, I just wanted to, you know," he stammered, eyes darting around, looking for a safe place to land that wasn't Zara.

A crinkling noise caught her attention; he was twisting a grubby paper bag in his hands.

"What's in the bag?"

"Oh, this?" he asked, momentarily confused. "Oh, right, this!" he brightened. He shoved the bag into the space between them. "It's for you."

She took it gingerly and peeked inside.

The box of pastels.

Looking down at Dave questioningly but trying to show approval in her face, she slid the precious art supplies out of their box and inspected them. They were all there, all in excellent condition.

She smiled in what she hoped was a sweet way and asked, "Why did you bring me these? I told Eric that I'd pay you for them."

Having no bag to twist his nerves out on, the boy rocked back and forth on his heels. "I was sort of hoping that, you know, you'd like them enough to…" his voice trailed off in an inaudible mutter.

"What?" Zara leaned forward automatically to hear better, closing the distance Dave had so carefully put between them.

"Swap me for a tattoo!" he yelped, jumping several steps back. He held his hands in front of his face as if expecting a beating. Zara wasn't sure if that was reflective of the home he'd run away from or another rumor she hadn't heard yet.

"Hey, c'mon," she said soothingly. The early-morning fuzz in her brain softened her edges, making her feel magnanimous. She reached out on impulse and took one of his hands. "Don't know what you heard about me, but smacking folks isn't really my thing. I'm much more of a silent-treatment kind of girl." She quirked half a smile at him.

Dave didn't see the joke. His hand trembled, making her wonder.

She said, "You came all the way down here at six thirty in the morning to give me presents and ask me for a favor, but you can't look me in the face?" She squeezed his hand and took a step closer. "C'mon, Dave. What's going on?"

He squirmed a little but didn't retreat again. "I saw what happened last week in the cafeteria," he said. "We all did. Most of us stayed up all night talking about it, and everybody wants to know if it'll work on them. I waited until the sun came up, but I couldn't wait anymore."

When he looked up at her for the first time, she could see something odd in his eyes. Fear mixed with hope? No one had ever looked at her like that before. There was a crowded moment of silent exchange between the two of them, the artist and the supplicant. And then the dam broke, and all his words rushed out in one long, breathless sentence.

"Mom and Dad didn't like that I kept failing my classes and my teachers all said I was broken and no one wanted to help me and no one would listen when I told them the words were all messed up and that I'm not stupid but they didn't care and would just whoop me with the belt when my report card came and one day the nurse saw and Dad got in trouble with the police and then it was the buckle when I got home and so I ran away and ended up here and I just want to be fixed so I can learn right and they'll love me again."

By the time he finished, gasping for breath, both of them had tears in their eyes. Zara didn't know what to do – she stood there, frozen, with his hand in hers, unsure of what to say. Thankfully, he filled in the gap for her.

"Zara, could you help me like you helped Sofi? Can you fix me with a tattoo?" It could've been the intense magnification of his glasses, but Zara would've sworn his eyes grew three sizes.

She hesitated.

Sofi was one thing, that was just a test run and no one could've foreseen those results. Would it be a good idea to work on other people? She'd consumed enough pop culture to know that magic gets out of control when shared with the wrong people. Bad shit happens.

She shouldn't have looked down into Dave's watery horn-rimmed eyes at that moment. If she hadn't done that, she could've said "no." But his story was etched in his retinas, inescapably true and pitiful. It cried out to her like the runt in the *Free Puppies* box outside a grocery store, begging to be swaddled up and cared for lest it be thrown in the dumpster.

Shit.

"Of course I'll help you," she said, her voice wavering only slightly.

The dark eyes lit up, and he let out an excited hoot, flinging both arms around her in a spontaneous hug. The moment solidified awkwardly – he wrapped around her, she rigid with shock – before he realized what he'd done. He broke off, blushing and muttering apologies as he backed away.

Zara stood there in Sofi's eye-searingly blue robe, still holding the offering of pastels as he skipped his way down the stairs, wondering exactly what she'd gotten herself into.

Meanwhile, six stories up from the Big Room, Agent 24 had been drooling onto a stack of classified documents. When the newest red light went live, a blaring siren sprang from his computer and slapped him out of a not-safe-for-work dream, the desk erupting in a flurry of damp paperwork as he flailed to shut off the alarm.

That's what you get for listening to dubstep remixes all night, he thought to himself as he cranked the speakers down.

He squinted at the computer monitor through sleep-hazy eyes at the system email. Volunteering for notification duty had seemed like a great move at the time, but after two weeks, he already regretted it. Between his usual secretaryesque assignments and the brown-nosing favors he'd been doing, this had pushed him too far. He'd been working 18-hour shifts like a 60+ agent but getting recognition like an under-20. Plus, his blood was now eighty percent taurine, his goldfish had all died, and his girlfriend wasn't sure he existed anymore. But, still. If you wanted to get ahead in this department, sacrifices had to be made. He could always get more fish.

Agent 24 rubbed his eyes and read the email again:

> From: System <sys@spdprivate.gov>
> To: Agent 24 <24@sdcprivate.gov>
> Subject: Anomaly Reported
> Time Registered: 1700 hours
> Agency Map Location: Sector 6, Quadrant 2
> Block Scale Rating: 7.8 of 10
> Threat Rating: 4 of 10
> Description: adolescent female, body modification, enchanted technology, unconscious/accidental
> Suggested Agents: Agent 67, Enchanted Technology; Agent 86, Abnormal Body Modification; Agent 97, Underage Specialist

He skimmed through the attached dossier, then read the email one more time, just to be sure. He sighed slightly, a mix between exhaustion and self-pity. Only one of those agents had the skills for that Block rating. And it wasn't the one he liked.

Agent 24 punched a series of codes into his workstation, sending out an email of his own and printing hard copies of the files. He guzzled another twelve ounces of hummingbird fuel for good measure, then stalked into the corridor towards the elevators. Time to officially assign the case.

Back in the Big Room, the light over Steeltown went out.

Few people ever expect to be famous, even if it is only in a 5,000 square foot radius. Certainly not scruffy adolescent runaways who shoplift from convenience stores and squat in an abandoned schoolhouse. But sometimes fame comes creeping along and jumps you in a blind alley when you're not looking.

The odd thing about Dave's tattoo was that he'd never told Zara what to draw. He'd wordlessly tugged off his shirt, hugged the reversed folding chair, and waited as goosebumps marched up his back, trusting she knew what she was doing. And the design just came to her, dropping effortlessly into her brain like one of those perfect ideas you have in the shower.

A dictionary. Unabridged-Oxford-English style. Heavy blue covers. Gold leaf. Membrane-thin pages. A peek into the middle.

It couldn't possibly be anything else.

A few ecstatic hours later, Zara was sprawled in her bed napping, and Dave was parked at the long table in the Heights' scanty library, surrounded by dusty volumes of classics and the occasional well-thumbed steamy romance novel, practically bursting with the sheer joy of words behaving themselves for the first time in his life.

That's how things got out of hand.

Despite Zara's admonitions of secrecy, the news of Dave's bravery shot through the residents of Runaway Heights like bottom-shelf vodka through a freshman and brought her a tidal wave of tattoo requests. By going first, he'd created the precedence for supplications. It seemed everyone had something they wanted to change about themselves that only Zara's magic inkpen could fix. Shrinking violets suddenly became outgoing socialites. Bouncing energy balls suddenly seemed focused and calm. Even lactose intolerance, body dysmorphia, and chronic procrastination melted under her touch.

The "inkchanger" legend practically built itself over the next two weeks as Zara spent exhaustive hours on commissions like some kind of mind-reading tattooing superhero. The rules were simple: You could ask her to do the work, but you couldn't talk to her, couldn't make requests, couldn't change her mind, and couldn't pay her. She'd just roll up your jeans or tug off your shirt and put the needle to your skin, falling into an rapturous trance for however long it took to finish. Whatever she created turned out to be precisely what you most needed, even if you hadn't known it at the time. When it was over, she'd be covered in a fine film of sweat, black hair a-tangle, orgasmic joy burning her cheeks. She'd flash you a smile and you'd leave in a bit of a daze, carrying a new you inside your skin, waiting to be born.

Before long, everyone had a unique tattoo, creating even tighter-knit community, bonded together with strength and ink instead of fear and misery. More basketball, less fist-fights; more cooperative runs, less pranking; more celebrations, less hiding. Each resident deftly sewed the inkpen's existence into their vows of silence about their adopted home. You kept the secrets of the Heights as much for the others as for yourself; if one person let anything slip, it could hurl the entire population back into the personal hells from which they had escaped. And since no one wanted strangers poking around the place and threatening their sanctuary, the magical tattoos logically fell under the confidential umbrella.

Even Zara had to admit to feeling more at home. She'd lived here for two years, but she'd never bothered to learn anyone's name and had actively avoided the common rooms. Now, when she walked through the halls, people smiled and chatted with her instead of scurrying away. They invited her to card games and took over her chores. She left her literal mark on every human soul who knocked on her door asking for help. Part of her was curled up in their skin, invisibly bonding them. She could feel them like feathers in a breeze, warm tingles in her mind if she sat still long enough. And, to even her surprise, she liked it; if only for a little while, she could pretend to be safe.

In between tattoo sessions one unseasonably-warm afternoon, Sofi and Zara headed to Gage Park to have a "who can swing the highest" contest, taking turns flinging themselves out of the seat at precarious heights and giggling. Sure, it was a little-kids' game, but they were riding high on the pixie stick fumes of strange and wonderful few weeks.

"Jump, dammit!" Sofi hollered across the gap between their swings. "Chickenshit!"

"Okay, okay! I'm going, I'm going!"

Zara pumped her legs harder and faster, the chains of the swing creaking their protest but still carrying her higher and higher. Narrowing her eyes, she focused all her willpower on a spot a few yards out in the soft grass. The mix of the rare moment of childish fun, plus the dangerous thrill of the jump filled her brain with the familiar cotton-candy fog.

She pumped a few more times for good measure, savoring the whoosh against her cheeks, and tensed every muscle she could think of. With an ear-piercing shriek of delight, she flung herself out of the rubber sling and sailed through the thin fall air as Sofi cheered. Zara landed clumsily with a soft *poomf*, then rolled a little ways in the dying grass to burn off the momentum, coming to a stop on her back.

"Awesome!" Sofi shouted. "My turn!"

Zara barely had time to squeal and curl into a protective ball before Sofi barreled out of the swing in her direction. She flew gracefully across the gravel, over the grass, and landed expertly balanced several feet on the other side of her friend. She flung out her arms and stuck out her chest like a proud gymnast sticking the dismount.

"Ta da!"

Zara chucked a hunk of uprooted turf at her. "You could've squished me!" she giggled.

Sofi grinned and offered her a hand, lifting the twiggy girl to her feet as easily as if she'd been a photograph of herself, and they scuttled back to the swings together.

After a few more rounds of the game, the sun dipped and their energy gave out as they tried to squeeze the last few minutes out of the day.

Zara looked towards the violently orange sunset over the grease-speckled bay and sighed, a mix of happiness and trepidation.

"What's up, Z?"

Another sigh.

"Come on, man. It's been a great day – don't ruin it by getting all emo on me now."

Zara twitched a wry smile. "That's just it, though. It really has been a great day. Great couple of weeks. But it's not enough, you know? Everybody's so freaking happy with their tattoos. Don't get me wrong, I love doing it, and I'm happy they're happy. But every night I go to bed and sit in the dark. Everybody got what they wanted except me."

Only the creak of rusty metal cut the silence for a long moment.

"Don't take this the wrong way," Sofi eventually said, "but why couldn't you just tattoo yourself? Seems pretty obvious."

Zara's brow furrowed. "I don't know what'll happen. The certainty I get when I'm inking other people isn't there. It just kinda feels... wrong."

"What, like holding up a guitar to an amp? Feedback?"

"Maybe. Some days I know for sure something awful would happen, like I'd grow roses for hands or burst into flames. Some days I get as far as turning the inkpen on before I chicken out." She shook her head. "I've even tried talking to the stupid thing, but I can't figure it out."

"Look at everyone else, though – we're all fine. I haven't mauled any tourists or stolen any picnic baskets."

"It's different. Somehow, it's just different."

Sofi huffed a little, more out of worry than annoyance. "Well, if you don't think it's worth the risk, don't do it. I bombed my seedling project in freshman science, and I have absolutely zero confidence that I can handle gardening a rose-girl with a black thumb like mine."

Zara gave Sofi a little laugh and smile that she didn't feel, then tilted her chin towards the Heights.

Best to get home before the night came and the darkness closed in again.

By the time Zara headed to her room, Sofi off in the cafeteria for dinner, she was so absorbed in thought that she didn't see the box in front of her door. It caught her unsuspecting toe and pitched her to the floor. Flinging out her hands and scrabbling at the nearby wall, she managed to slow her fall but still landed face-first next to the offending obstacle.

From this vantage point, even through the stars she was seeing, she had a fantastic view of the intricate carvings that covered the dark-stained wood. Brambles and stems and thorns and rosebuds. The heavy lid was held shut with a worn brass latch, and the entire thing had the slightly-off glow of the handmade.

And there was a scrap of cream-colored paper sticking out of it.

Curious, she pushed herself up on one elbow but didn't bother to peel herself off the floor. Nobody was around to see her, anyway. She lifted the edge of the box and slid out the note written in a careful, slow hand.

> *Z: Thought you might want a treasure chest to keep your prize possession safe. – (notable lack of Xs and Os) Eric*

The smile crept across her lips unbidden. She let it linger a while before demolishing it. A thoughtful present, true. But a wooden box, no matter how beautifully or lovingly made, wasn't nearly enough to dent the armor around her heart.

She wondered if anything ever would be.

A place for everything, and everything in its place. Looking around the room, it seemed the saying was invented just for Agent 97.

A visitor could've easily mistaken the clinically sterile room for a doctor's office rather than the office of the third-best member of the ultra-top-secret Supernatural Cases Department of the FBI. Most other agents' offices looked lived-in, an accurate description given that many slept curled up under their desks at least three nights a week. Some even had tiny mattresses and refrigerators fitted. The average working space for an SCD employee was decorated with important personal touches that reminded the resident of their humanity: family photos, succulent plants, zen rock gardens. You needed an anchor to the mundane world in this job, lest you forget yourself. The records were filled with accounts of agents who'd leapt off bridges thinking they could fly after too many encounters with fairies and not enough pictures of Monday-hating puppies in their office.

    And so walking into Agent 97's office came as a bit of a shock to anyone who visited. He had requested it painted nursing-home beige to cut down on glare, removed the previous occupant's biography-filled bookshelves, and installed blackout shades over the only source of natural light; his only additions to the room were a starched army cot and a closet filled with seven identical suits. Behind the standard-issue ergonomic chair, a geometrically-aligned array of framed certificates quietly showed the world Agent

97's dedication to his department. "Most Evasive Congressional Testimony" held a place of pride in the center. The fluorescent bulbs buzzing softly in the ceiling illuminated a Spartan desk: an antiquated computer, a legal pad with silver pen, and a single picture frame. No other agent had ever seen the contents of the frame, and there was a betting pool as to what could possibly be in there. A picture of his ex-wife? His cat? The president? Agent Smith from *The Matrix*?

The only sound in Agent 97's office was the incessant tapping of the keyboard as he filed his paperwork. On days he did leave the office, it was never before 1900; he attacked the unending sea of reports as if they were a personal affront. By 1830, he had nearly won – just one more PD24 to go and he'd sleep easier tonight.

Two things happened simultaneously: a gentle *ping* on his computer screen and a tentative knock on his glass door.

Anomaly Reported in Sector 6, Quadrant 2.

"Agent 97, you in there?" asked the visitor, fidgeting with the manila folder he was carrying. Agent 24 knew full well that he was, but he didn't dare just walk in. The last guy who did that had to go home and phone his mother for reassurance that he was still a valuable human being.

"Come."

Agent 24 gingerly pushed open the door with his empty hand and took the only seat in front of the wide desk. Agent 97 had pulled up the computer's report and was scanning through it, the email's reflection on his ubiquitous sunglasses showing Agent 24 that he'd probably wasted his time. He might have to complain to someone in admin about sending runners (i.e.: him) to give paper documents to agents when they already had digital ones. Then again, he could probably use the exercise.

The visiting agent slid the dossier onto the pristine desk and waited to be acknowledged. Agent 97 took another solid five minutes to finish his reading, then picked up the paper report and took another ten to flip through that, despite it containing exactly the same information.

Agent 24 couldn't help noticing, in his meditative silence, how fresh-pressed Agent 97 looked; the man never had a wrinkle, piece of lint, or hint of dandruff on him. Like a well-oiled machine.

That guy ain't right.

When Agent 97 finally deigned to speak to him, it was in the flat tones of the unimpressed. Not that he ever used a different one.

"It appears that this case is better suited for Agent 86 as she is in charge of Abnormal Body Modification." The senior agent's shielded gaze fixed on the messenger, making him squirm slightly. "Can you explain why this case was brought to my attention, Agent 24?"

The younger man smiled nervously, showing too many teeth, and pointed back to the glass door. "The teenagers, sir. You're our Underage Anomalies Specialist, after all. The tech in this case isn't obscure enough to warrant Agent 67, and Agent 86 isn't exactly the most...," he searched for the right words, "...understanding person. It'd be like using a chainsaw to mow the lawn."

He instantly knew he'd made a mistake. He groaned inwardly and braced himself.

Agent 97 froze into a wax statue of himself, the contemplative gears of his mind nearly audible as the description fought for understanding in the blasted wasteland that used to be his imagination. But the simple image was no match for reality's stark, sinister weapons; it died an ignoble death among husks of greater metaphors.

Eventually, his features reanimated, and he said, "Surely, using a chainsaw to maintain one's lawn would achieve the desired outcome, albeit with additional required effort and an undesirable aesthetic." Pause. "What do the chainsaw and the lawn have to do with this case, Agent 24?"

"Nothing, sir. Just a figure of speech."

"I see," Agent 97 said flatly. "Perhaps in the future, Agent 24, you could make the effort to utilize practical speech rather than relying on abstract concepts to make yourself understood. This department is no place for the frivolous or overly imaginative. Such whimsy is the first warning sign that preventative psychological treatment is required." He tilted his head ever so slightly but didn't actually look over the edge of his sunglasses. "I trust that you understand the implications."

Agent 24 swallowed hard, willing nonexistent spit to keep his voice from squeaking. "Yes, sir, understood." You don't argue with a nearly-seven-foot-tall man in a thousand-dollar suit, no matter who you are.

"Excellent." Agent 97 snapped the folder shut. "That will be all, Agent 24. I appreciate you taking time out of your undoubtedly busy day to provide me with this information. Please inform Agent 100 that I will be leaving at nineteen-oh-seven hours to investigate the anomaly and bring in Miss Zara Carter for questioning and debriefing."

Done with the exchange, Agent 97 folded his hands neatly on the desk and stared stoically ahead, pointedly ignoring Agent 24. The younger man didn't need to be told twice; he was out and the door shut behind him in seconds. Besides, there was a bottle in his desk that wouldn't drink itself.

Agent 97 had been with the SCD for over ten years. And when you're a specialist on teenagers and children for a supernatural investigation unit, you're privy to some of the most awesome and most terrifying anomalies in the world. He'd logged over three hundred cases – twice that of anyone of his tenure – and each one held its own brand of magic, its own variety of horror. Sitting at his desk, scanning over Z. Carter's file, he couldn't help recalling past cases. A toddler whose crayon drawings came to life. A pre-pubescent boy afflicted with vampirism. A teen mother whose unborn baby gave her precognitive abilities. Thankfully, SCD training gave its agents the one useful defense against supernatural encounters: disbelief, the ability to see what's really there.

      He hadn't exaggerated when he'd warned Agent 24 about fanciful imagery. The instant an agent got caught up in magical thinking and found themselves buying into the bizarre circumstances of a case, they were lost. Having an imagination could get you killed in this job; worse, it could have you *believing* these people were normal citizens. To be an effective agent, you had to be solid and unwavering in the knowledge that seemingly supernatural phenomenon have completely logical explanations. You had to not just accept but *know* that these aberrations had to be carefully studied and corrected for the betterment of the world at large. You were grounded and logical at all costs in this department, lest your next case find you following

Queen Mab (on the books for human trafficking and substance abuse) into another dimension where no amount of disbelief could rescue you.

When he was a greenhorn, Agent 97 heard whispered legends of agents who lost their grip on reality and wandered off after a suburban unicorn or nefarious dryad, never to return. The stories had more than their desired effect on him; rather than simply being cautious, he used every ounce of his titanic willpower to erase any traces of childish imagination left to him by his twenties. Much as a smoker actively reprograms themselves into believing they simply don't want a cigarette, Agent 97 worked daily to eradicate fantasy from his world, replacing soft metaphor with hard logic. He'd be damned if his career – or life - would end because he couldn't tell the difference between a changeling and a human child. It was a slow, painstaking process, but that was exactly the sort of work he liked, and the tactic served him well. He rose through the ranks of the FBI and SCD like an... unexpectedly fast thing. He impressed his superiors so greatly with his dedication and focus that he became the youngest 97 in history at age 35.

And this tattoo case would be the final touch on the masterpiece of his career.

He shifted his shaded eyes to the picture frame on his desk. Rather than the much-gossiped-about alternatives, it held a flowchart showing all one hundred department agents in their proper hierarchy. There were no pictures and no names – no one in the department had one anymore – only numbers and lines. Although Agent 97 had successfully expunged his imagination, a tiny scrap had fled for its life, desperately pouring itself into the closest available container: ambition. This constant visual reminder fueled him to straddle the final three slots and become the greatest Agent 100 ever. He allowed himself a rare smile as he indulged this moment of fancy. *Someday.*

Having fulfilled his paperwork obligations and given himself two full minutes of his daily allotted "personal hour," Agent 97 stepped to his modest closet near the front of the office. Opening the slick laminate door revealed seven sets of too-neat clothing and a pre-packed black duffle filled with additional suits and assorted traveling necessities. Where other agents preferred to travel incognito on a case, he insisted on wearing his black-suit, white-shirt uniform at all times. If you had to disguise yourself in pursuit of your duty, you weren't ready for field work.

He slung the duffle easily over his shoulder, insinuated himself out of the office, and locked the door, his polished wingtips clicking as he headed to the garage.

It was 1907 on the dot when he pulled into traffic.

"We've got six cases of clam chowder, two vegetable beef, and three old-fashioned chicken noodle."

Eric was knee-deep in the soup section of the Heights' storage room late that afternoon, counting up all the new stock. Anything they could possibly have wanted was in here: pasta, snack cakes, toilet paper, meds, even fresh fruit. The magically-tattooed residents had settled into their gifts and were bursting with confidence; as a result, the last month had seen this room overflow with record-breaking c-store treasures. Everyone seemed to recognize the new cords of community at the same time, making big plans for sprucing up and reorganizing the building itself to create the right extended-family vibe.

Right now, though, there was work to be done in the pantry. Zara had volunteered to help Eric do the monthly inventory check, which surprised the crap out of him. He'd gotten so used to her flagrant rejections that he wasn't quite sure how to react to this sort of friendliness. He didn't know if he was being invited to make a move or just getting a bit of guilt-free labor. He opted to go with the latter just to be safe.

But something was clearly different about Zara. In the last few weeks, she'd gone from an angry ball of ratty hair and a matching temper to a poised and smooth, if still slightly reclusive, artist. Her stride was just a bit longer, her head tilted just a bit higher. Even her last few paintings had been more vibrant. Popularity agreed with her.

Maybe things were different enough now...

"Hey, Z," he said, screwing up his abused courage. "Wanna grab something to eat that didn't come out of a box?" He winced at a teen-boy squeak as he rushed over the words.

Silence.

Bracing for the all-too-familiar rebuff, he opened his mouth to say it was okay, he understood, it was cool, she didn't have to, when she replied: "Yeah, sure. Let's go to The Egg; they're always open. I could seriously use a greasy diner breakfast right about now."

He snapped his head around, surprised, and threw himself a little off balance. Maybe he was dreaming? Although, if it was that one dream, he shouldn't be wearing pants.

"Really?" he said incredulously.

Up on the ladder, Zara laughed as she stowed the two boxes of cookies she'd been holding. "Really, really."

She hopped down and gave him a smile, all teeth and sweetness. No hint of either promise or guilt there, just a good friend agreeing to have dinner with another good friend. At least, that's what Eric made himself see. No use in getting all wound up just yet.

"How about if I meet you there in, say, an hour?" he said, trying desperately to shove his excitement out of sight. "I gotta find my good shirt and, you know, clean it." He plucked at the grimy work beater he'd been wearing for emphasis. "See you there!" he chimed, nearly bouncing out the door, completely forgetting to pick up his Mountain Dew stash.

It's one of the great female mysteries of life: no matter how big or small your wardrobe, the instant you care about what you're wearing, there's nothing to wear. Zara was up to her eyeballs in her dresser right now, and Sofi was trying hard not to laugh as she agonized over whether to pair a brown sweater with black jeans.

"Are you sure it's not a date?" asked Sofi from her bed.

"For the millionth time, yes! Why do you keep asking me that?"

"Cos you're angsting like you're going to prom with Johnny Depp, not getting food with someone you refuse to like."

Zara huffed melodramatically. "It's not a date. Dates are all puppy dog eyes over a milkshake with two straws and shit like that. I'm hungry, and Eric just happened to suggest going out, that's all."

"Uh-huh."

"What is with you, Soph?" Zara said, her voice muffled by the green turtleneck she was pulling on.

Sofi rolled onto her back so her blonde hair brushed the floor. "Me? I'm just an amused bystander." She grew a knowing grin.

Zara huffed again and turned, arms out for inspection. "What do you think? Passably human?"

Sofi popped up and walked full circle around her, casting a critical eye over the ensemble. Olive green turtleneck, used-to-be-white tee, slightly torn black jeans, brown shit-kicking boots. Suitably presentable, yet punk. Very "I like you but I don't like you."

"Well, you can dress yourself, apparently, but I'll be damned if I'm letting you go out with your hair looking like that."

Sofi gently pushed the protesting hairball down onto her bed and began the arduous process of pulling a brush through her mat of black hair. *Leave it to Momma Bear to give you a spit bath just before you head out.*

Eric.

As she walked through the last of the autumn leaves in the sinking twilight, Zara hoped he wasn't getting the wrong idea. She'd agreed to come out before she realized he'd think it was a date; she just wanted to get some fresh air and had jumped at the chance to hit The Egg. But she'd seen the excitement flash in his green eyes when she'd said yes. Maybe she'd made a mistake.

Then again, she wasn't sure it was the wrong idea. She'd sketched his high cheekbones and long legs in secret notebooks during endless insomnia-wracked nights. She loved watching him charm the newbie runaways, effortlessly putting them at ease and helping them settle in; the way he cared for every sideways-looking kid that wandered through the door threatened to melt the icebergs in her veins. Even with his penchant for rake-in-the-crotch humor and his questionable diet, he'd so very nearly won her over. Fierce kindness, gentle strength, elfin good looks – how could she resist that?

Too many years of broken trust and abandonment, too many people pretending to love me then crushing me. That's how. Almost too easy. Even with the inkpen, this long-frozen lock hasn't budged; that stalwart guardian corrals my everything into that lonely oubliette and refuses to abandon his post until the coast is absolutely, positively, without a doubt clear. Catch-22: no love without risk, risk means death, and love means death, means no Eric. The coast will never be clear.

Despite the fugue settling over her head, the awareness that something was wrong crept along Zara's spine the closer she got to the restaurant. She knew she was early, but that was intentional; she didn't like being waited on. As she opened The Egg's steel door, she could see her usual booth was taken, not by Twitch - the local speed junkie who liked to camp there with his Spider-Man sleeping bag – but by a too-clean man in a suit so sharp he'd probably had cut himself getting into it. The sleek black hair, leather gloves, spotless shoes, and opaque sunglasses made him stick out worse than if he'd been wearing a clown suit and juggling goslings. He didn't get up or take off his shades, only gestured for her to take the opposite seat.

"Hello, Miss Carter. I am Agent 97. I've been waiting for you."

Thirty seconds later, against her better judgment, Zara was rooted to the cold plastic booth, listening to this creepy man in black telling her every detail of her own life story.

"Your mother, an elementary school art teacher, and your father, a middle-rank investment banker, died in a single-car accident at mile 54 on Highway Two when you were ten. Your eight-year-old brother succumbed to internal injuries of the liver and lungs one week later in the children's wing of Steeltown General Hospital. You were inexplicably unhurt. You had no close relatives capable of housing you; therefore, you were entered into the foster care system immediately. Over the course of the next six years, you were ejected from four foster homes due to physical or sexual abuse by a foster parent, three due to unfit environment, and three for officially 'unspecified' reasons but were actually because you actively sabotaged your relationship with your hosts.

"At age sixteen, you left your foster home and failed to return to classes at John A. McDonald High School. You now live in an abandoned schoolhouse in the north end of Steeltown, commonly called 'Runaway Heights' by its residents, of which there are twenty-five, aged twelve to twenty-two. You have largely refused to matriculate until very recently. Your primary companions are Miss Sofi Strella and Mister Eric Weaver.

"Between petty larceny, breaking and entering, and trespassing offenses, you enjoy a reputation as a skilled painter among the wealthy residents of Steeltown. You have recently expanded your repertoire after discovering a tattooing device commonly known as an 'inkpen.' It is your interaction with this mechanism that has brought me here today."

Zara sat there, eyes wide, but pretending as hard as she could that she wasn't scared of this asshole and that she didn't care what he knew about her. She wasn't doing a very good job; the hamster wheel of worry was spinning wildly. To hide her distress, she put on her best "fuck you" face, the one she saved for patronizing cops and nosy art collectors.

"Anybody with access to court records and pocket full of twenties could find out that stuff," she scoffed. "You're gonna have to do better."

Agent 97's expression didn't change. He wordlessly shuffled a few papers in the folder on the table and pulled out a glossy oversized photograph.

Sofi on a run, carrying a military rucksack filled to overflowing, her sleeveless shirt clearly displaying the bear paw tattoo.

And another.

Zara working on a Heights kid at the school's playground, her face beaming, a little crowd gathered around.

And another.

Zara and Sofi in the cafeteria of the Heights – this one taken only a couple of days ago, right through the window.

"What the fuck is this?" she said hoarsely, dropping the tough-girl façade. "Who are you?"

"I am Agent 97. I work for the Supernatural Cases Department of the FBI. These surveillance photographs are part of your case file. Your recent anomalous activities have brought you to our attention, and I have been instructed to bring you back to the agency for questioning and debriefing. You will not be allowed to return to your domicile or communicate with any other individuals, for security reasons. This measure is for your protection and for the continued well-being of our society."

"Fuck that!" Zara spat. A testament to the clientele, no one in the diner batted an eye. "What, so you can torture me and carve up my brain?"

Agent 97 remained impassive, his hands folded neatly on the table. "Miss Zara Carter: I am formally requesting that you surrender yourself peacefully and without hesitation. Your activities are a level four threat to national security and cannot be allowed to continue unchecked. I strongly recommend that you acquiesce to my request. Should you refuse to accompany me peacefully, there will be potentially harmful consequences to yourself," he said levelly, "and to the others upon whom you have utilized your questionable talents." It was a promise, not a threat.

Zara's mind raced. She only had a second or two to choose, she knew. Go along quietly and disappear forever into a straightjacket or fight for her freedom and warn everyone.

She chose.

"Fuck. You."

She bolted from the booth and sprinted, her hands hitting the door so hard the glass spiderwebbed.

Agent 97 didn't twitch a muscle as his quarry escaped. He watched her pound down the sidewalk back to her bolt-hole with vague interest, then gathered up the glossies from the table, neatly rearranging the case file. He wasn't worried. She'd chosen to do things the hard way, and now he was officially in hot pursuit.

At least he would be, right after breakfast.

He picked up a greasy menu with two gloved fingers as if it carried an infectious disease. He scanned it quickly and called out to the kitchen where Gladys was pretending not to eavesdrop on the conversation. "Coffee. Black. Two pieces of dry toast. Rye."

And then he waited. He had plenty of time.

Zara didn't look back as she fled the diner. She knew that fucking suit would still be sitting there, hands crossed, waiting. As much as she wanted him to be, he was definitely not a hallucination. Her brain kicked into overdrive as her legs carried her mindlessly back to the Heights.

How did he know? Oh, god, what did I do? What am I?

All entry protocol forgotten, she sprinted across the Heights' parched lawn and hit the foyer at full tilt, making the double doors scream in protest. Sweat ran down her back as she flew up the stairs to the dormitories.

Sofi was napping when Zara burst into their room, panting like a greyhound, hair and eyes wild. The door banged back against the wall like a gunshot, rocketing Sofi out of a dead sleep and to her feet, hands slashing the air in classic karate-chop action.

When she saw Zara, she relaxed, but only slightly.

"Jesus Christ, Z, what the fuck happened to you?"

"I think I just met Agent Mulder," Zara heaved. She hunched over in the doorway, elbows bent, head hanging at knee-level, trying to catch her breath. Between setting the record for the thousand-yard dash and the nauseating idea that she might be some kind of mutant, her stomach hadn't decided whether or not it would be a good idea to barf.

Confused but concerned, Sofi sidled up and gently led Zara over to her bed, pushing the door closed with her toes. She squatted down to look at her friend, who had buried her fingers in her tangled mane and was staring at the threadbare carpet.

"What happened?" she repeated.

"I don't know. But he had pictures of all of us." Zara shook her head. Her eyes shone with unshed tears. "He said he was from some special FBI department and had to take me in. Said I was a 'threat to national security' or some shit."

"How is that even possible?"

Zara's gaze fell on the hand-carved box stowed in the bookshelf. It tugged at her in a half-conscious place, begging to be used and electrifying the ends of her fingers with its familiar call, but she angrily shook it off.

"It's got to be the tattoos," she croaked. "He called me an anomaly. Like I'm some kind of freak. Like I'm dangerous."

Sofi's entire body tensed with defensive instinct. "What else?"

She looked down guiltily. "When I wouldn't come along, he threatened me. And the Heights."

"He knows where we are?" Sofi said, her voice going up an octave. They weren't exactly living in Fort Knox, but still.

"One of the pics was shot right through the cafeteria window. I don't know how else they could've got it."

After a long pause, she said. "I don't think it's safe for me to stay here, Soph. He'll come after me, and I don't want anybody else getting caught up in this."

Wobbly but determined, she stood up and started to pull out the drawers of her dresser. She threw her scant collection of clothing onto her bed, followed by an extra pair of shoes, a fistful of art supplies, and the contents of the coffee can bank. When she went to the bookshelf for her prized crime novels, she hesitated. The buzzing in her fingertips redoubled as she reached past the inkpen's resting spot, it mentally whining at her to let it come along. But she wasn't having it.

No. You've caused enough trouble. You stay here where you can't do any more damage. Be broken forever without me. It's what you deserve.

As she crossed the room to get her backpack, Sofi stopped her.

"Hey, you can't seriously be leaving."

"What else am I supposed to do?" Zara pushed past her and pulled a weather-worn backpack out of the closet. "Haven't you ever seen a single movie? 'Taking you in for questioning' means they're going torture you. And if I really *am* some kind of magical freak, you can fucking bet they're going to cut me open to figure out how I work."

She threw the bag on the bed and angrily spun around. "Do you want that to happen?"

Sofi held up her hands defensively. "No!" she said. "But maybe this isn't like that. I mean, that's just movies, right? No way that shit happens for real. Maybe this guy is just trying to help you out."

"How?" Zara asked incredulously.

"Maybe they send you to X-Men school," she suggested. "If they're specialists, it can't just be automatic dissection or solitary confinement for life. Wouldn't they want to preserve your gift? Use it for the greater good?"

A hesitant knock at the door cut off Zara's retort.

The girls looked at each other in alarm for a moment before Sofi pointed Zara back to the bed, out of range of the door. She reached down and gripped a heavy wooden baseball bat leaning against the wall, then carefully turned the knob with one hand, sliding the weapon behind her back with the other.

The door cracked an inch to reveal shaggy white-blonde hair.

"Soph, have you seen Zara?" Eric asked.

Both girls deflated with relief.

Sofi pulled the door back the rest of the way and gestured in Zara's direction. A little intimidated by the bat, Eric stayed in the doorway out of respect, but he was clearly pissed off.

"What the hell, Z? When I got to The Egg, you weren't there. Even Gladys said she hadn't seen you,"

Eric said. "I waited a while, but I figured you'd stood me up."

Zara couldn't speak. Her eyes welled up again, and her hands twisted in the straps of her backpack. She looked helplessly at Sofi, willing her to be her voice.

"You didn't see a guy in a black suit there?" Sofi asked.

"Uh, yeah, actually. Dude looked like he fell out of a bad FBI movie."

Zara groaned.

"And you didn't talk to him or anything?"

"No. Why - should I have?"

Sofi sighed heavily and pulled Eric into the room, closing the door behind him. She kept the bat, though; the weight of it was comforting.

Deep breath.

"Zara ran into a secret agent at The Egg saying he's some kind of special forces and he wants to take her in because of national security. We're pretty sure it's tattoo-related. He knows about the Heights and sort of threatened to do bad things if Z doesn't go with him. But she ran back here instead and is trying to escape so nobody else gets hurt." She paused to think. "Yeah, I think that covers it."

Eric's eyes bulged, his mouth hanging open as he processed the information. It took a minute before he said anything, but when he did, it was like he'd gotten a unicorn for Christmas.

"It's all real, then. The supernatural investigations unit, the magic conspiracy. Holy. Fucking. Shit. I can't wait to tell the guys on the message board! I'm going to be fucking famous!"

Sofi shoved a hard finger into the center of his chest, pushing him back a couple of inches. "Don't even fucking think about it, buddy. This is dangerous shit. Aren't you even slightly worried about the Heights?" She half-turned and pointed back at Zara. "Or her?"

That brought him back. Embarrassed, he rubbed the bruise he could feel blooming on his skin and looked at Zara. Fear radiated off her. And here he was thinking about being a hotshot conspiracy guru. Jackass.

"Wait," he said to Sofi, "What about the Heights? I can see why he'd be after Zara – no offense, Z – but nobody here has done anything worth this guy's time."

Zara cut in, her voice strained, "Could've been a bluff, but I get the feeling it's an either/or situation. Either he gets me or he'll take down the Heights. Punishment." She held up her bag. "So, I figured I'd run for it. He can chase me for a while and that'll give everybody time to get away, in case he comes back."

Eric held up a hand to silence Sofi's protest. Everyone always thought he was a crackpot for believing in men in black and Bigfoot, but now he had authority. *Not so crazy after all, eh?*

"You're right, Z," he said. "If he really is one of these special department guys, it's you he's after. The Heights wouldn't be in his orders, so he probably can't deal with us until you're resolved, even if he wanted to." A pained expression. "You running while we circle the wagons is probably the best plan for everybody."

"What?!" Sofi screeched. "You can't be serious!" She choked up on the bat still in her hands as if she could beat the idea out of existence.

Eric took a few steps backwards, arms raised protectively. "Whoa! Hey, it's just logic. If Z leads the agent away, we can make sure everyone here is safe. Plus, if she gets started now, the odds of him catching her are slim. He's probably still at The Egg waiting for her to turn herself in."

The bear girl lowered the bat and looked from Eric to Zara and back again, defeat creeping over her. She could see the fear and sureness in both their faces. And she didn't have a better plan – everything she could think of involved massacring federal agents. Slumping down onto her own bed, she took a deep breath, then let it out in a rush.

"Okay, fine," she conceded. "What do you think we should do, then, Mister Tinfoil Hat?"

"Seems like the best idea would be for Z to get a car and head north. If you cross the border, you're out of his jurisdiction, at least for a while."

Zara had been totally silent as her brain whirred, trying to remember something important. And when the word "border" snuck past her ears, it fell into place.

Without saying a word, she slowly walked to the back of the room where the formidable Mount Laundry had reestablished its reign over lesser messes. She pushed over a foothill of unmentionables to reveal a National Geographic map thumbtacked to the plaster. Eric and Sofi exchanged a curious glance, then joined her.

Zara had drawn all over topographic North America. She'd added twisting highways, unnatural landmarks, and gaudy tourist traps to the fading paper; she'd even scrawled "here there be dragons" over a mountain range. Looking more closely, though, Sofi noticed that the crayon additions formed a pattern. No, not a pattern: a route. It started with a bright pink star in Steeltown and wound its dotted-purple trail directly north, past the suburbs, around the hills, through the thick pine forest, avoided the major cities, and ended somewhere in the broad plains of midwestern Canada, another bright pink star at the end over a town whose name had been colored over too well to read.

Sofi smiled to herself; all this time living together and she'd never known Zara wanted to travel.

Without warning, she reached over and pulled Zara into a full embrace, which startled her. The terrified girl instinctively recoiled from the touch, but the sweetness of it made her soften. She couldn't remember the last time she'd been genuinely hugged and allowed it.

"It'll be okay, Z," Sofi reassured her. "I'm here, Eric's here, we're all here. No one's going to let anything happen to you, okay?"

She pulled herself together enough to hug back. "I know you are, Soph. Thanks."

Eric stood a bit awkwardly off to the side as the girls emoted on each other and examined the route, calculations ticking away in his mechanic's mind. It wouldn't be enough to have Zara sneak away into the night. She'd need a fast car. And some backup.

"Ladies," he said quietly. "I believe I've got a plan."

Zara twisted the key in the uncooperative ignition for the fourth time, her eyes flicking apprehensively around the crowded college parking lot to check for rent-a-cops and night students coming back to their cars. None had turned up in the fifteen minutes she'd been skulking around, trying door handles and looking for keys left in glove compartments or sun visors. This is where all the space-case kids went when they couldn't get into a good university: close to home, cheap tuition, easy classes. After rash of break-ins last year, increased lot security in the form of gates and guards had only made students more lackadaisical about locking up; it had only taken three tries to find what she needed. But it wasn't cooperating.

"Start. C'mon, start. Start goddamn you!"

Zara banged her head on the steering wheel as the outdated red sedan sputtered and coughed. This was definitely the riskiest part of Eric's escape plan, but they needed two vehicles for it to work, and Sofi couldn't hotwire a toaster, much less a car. That left Zara with grand theft auto while Eric supplied the other girl with an easier getaway.

But of course she'd picked a car with engine trouble. She swore at it in a way usually reserved for middle-aged men watching a hockey game.

Vroooooom! RUnnnnnnUnnnnnUnnn.

"Yes!" Zara cheered, pumping her fist and nearly losing her traction on the gas. The car shuddered and the headlights flickered. She slammed her foot back. "Sorry! Don't die on me now."

She buckled in and shifted into reverse. As she reached to adjust the rearview, she spotted a dark-blue streak of movement under a lamp post.

Shit.

The security guard's uniform strained to contain him, the metal tines of various zippers hanging on for dear life. But Officer Andy had been tracking this scruffy vagrant since she wandered into the lot, and he'd be damned if he was going to let her make off with a car under his protection. He'd hoped she was looking for a quick smash 'n' grab –he could let that slide, pretending he'd been very busy indeed with important security guard business – but a car goes missing, that's him on the dole.

Zara saw him closing and jammed her foot to the floor, squealing the tires and narrowly missing the pickup truck behind her. The guard shouted incoherently, red-faced with the effort of his clumsy chase, and made a lateral move towards a security shed at the mouth of the parking lot to lower the gate arm.

Moves pretty fast for a donut-muncher, she mused to herself as she jammed the shifter into drive.

The car lurched forward and spun past three rows of cowering vehicles, heading directly for the exit. She could see the guard squeezing into the prefab booth and flapping around frantically to find the lowering mechanism for the gate. She grinned, adrenaline brimming in her brain, and watched the revs climb higher, propelling her towards freedom.

Inside the booth, Officer Andy cursed himself for not paying better attention on orientation day. The crossword puzzle had seemed so much more interesting at the time. Now that he was in here, all the dials looked the same, and none of them were marked. *Who the fuck runs this thing, Stevie Wonder?!*

He slammed a chapped fist down on a random button and a siren went off inside the booth. *Motherfucker!*

He chose a toggle switch this time, and the radio blared to life. *Shitbuckets!*

He could see a red streak flitting through pools of lamp light and knew he only had time for one more try. At the exact moment the siren and song matched up in ear-splitting harmony, he brought his hand down on a big green button and gritted his teeth.

The bar started to move.

"Come on, you cocksucking fuckface!" he screamed at the machine, certain his mother's ears were burning. "Can't you go any faster?!"

It couldn't.

Zara screamed wild encouragement at her vehicle, high on the action-movie moment. The elderly vehicle cheerfully complied, just as anxious to be free as she was. They zoomed up and out of the gated driveway just as the creaky yellow bar closed down over the rear bumper. The scrape of metal lasted only a second, then they were gone, leaving nothing but a black skid mark on the pavement as Zara raced to meet up with Sofi on the outskirts of town.

Officer Andy slumped in his miniature box of shame. At least the music was decent.

She'd made it to the highway and was well into the suburbs before her brain quit hummingbirding and she could think straight again. Barring the dramatic beginning, Zara reflected that the escape had gone relatively well. She'd managed to acquisition a car, had picked up a mountain of junk food, and found enough cash for a few tanks of gas. At least she wasn't in jail.

An annoying thought niggled at her brain, reminding her that she hadn't seen Sofi yet. They'd opted to split up while Zara boosted her ride, but they were supposed to meet at the gas station at the city limits, right where things turned back into countryside. Eric had said traveling in separate cars would make it easier to lose any black SUVs tailing them; he seemed to know what he was talking about, so they hadn't argued. Plus, he was risking his own neck by staying behind with the Heights kids in case any secret agents turned up. Zara had to respect that. But she'd waited as long as she dared at the station with no sign of Sofi. That had her worried, but she talked herself into pushing on anyway.

Sofi can take care of herself. Probably just got caught up saying goodbye to the Heights. Eric will make sure she gets what she needs.

For now, it was just her, the red sedan, and the open road. She could see the map of the journey perfectly in her mind. The ocean-eroded coastline, the jagged edge of the evergreen mountains, and the spaghetti knotwork of highways that would take her all the way to the Great White North. A swirl of girlish charm and the roar of an engine at the border, and she'd be safe, alone and free in a new place. Somewhere so far away that maybe even a low-life iceberg like her could find answers and maybe even some hope.

When she'd planned it as a little girl, it was just an idea, a happy place where she could hide from the horrors of being alone in a world that didn't care what happened to her. Now it was real, a desperate escape route etched into her memory with the acid of fear. Strange to think that it took being hunted by the FBI to set her on the road trip she'd been dreaming of for all those years.

The sun had started go to down by the time she reached the edge of the suburbs, casting wine-colored shadows along the dying grass. It had been a breeze of a drive; she'd only seen one or two cars in the last half hour or so, and there was no sign of the fuzz. All that lay before her now was a few hundred miles of open highway. Over the river, through the woods. But first, the misty mountains. She took a deep breath and sighed with a mixture of contentedness and regret. Whether or not she'd ever see Steeltown again was a mystery, but it was one the whine of tires on asphalt might be able to alleviate.

She crested the last hill before the unending flatness of the freeway and leaned into the bend of the exit.

"Fuck!"

Zara slammed on the brakes and jerked the wheel hard to the right as far as it would go. Smoke poured from the tires as she sailed through an evasive move that any James Bond stuntman would've been proud of. The noise would've punctured her eardrums if the blood pounding through her head hadn't already deafened her. She gripped the steering wheel with both hands, white-knuckled and still screaming. The car seemed to be endlessly revolving, taking years to come to a jerky sideways halt across the two-lane road.

Panting heavily, head spinning and lungs heaving, she convinced her eyelids to open one at a time and see what was blocking the road.

A single black SUV. A tall, thin man in a too-perfect suit. Both cinematically silhouetted against the blazing autumn sun, neither seeming to cast a shadow.

"You've got to be shitting me."

Agent 97 didn't move, just stood by the passenger side door of his standard-FBI-issue vehicle blocking both lanes, hands folded studiously at waist level, the headlights of Zara's car reflected in his shades.

Minutes crawled by as if trying to escape unnoticed. The sun, already slipping from its perch, continued its lazy descent until the shadows melted into the night sky. In a sort of reverse event, the idea dawned on Zara that Agent 97 was waiting for her to get out of the car. Close on the heels of that realization came one saying there was absolutely no traffic, coming or going. She was alone out here. And he was waiting.

Options, options – what are my options?

Turn myself in? *Yeah, no.*

Run back home? Hide in the Heights? No way.

Mow him down and make a run for it? Then I'm actually a felon.

And what if you don't take him out? Think he's going to stop looking for you? I mean, seriously – he found you out here. I was being sarcastic, but it's probably your best option. Maybe you could just, like, fake it. Zoom up on him, then swerve off? That oughta scare him enough to give you a good head start.

Although she wasn't entirely sure who she was arguing with – she didn't want to think about the possibility of suddenly acquiring a personality disorder – she had to agree. The only way out was forward, and Agent 97 was in her way.

The sedan had been idling fitfully during the standoff, threatening to sputter and die if it didn't get some attention, and it responded with gusto when she put pressure on the gas. She revved the engine hard in warning, the ripsnort of a bull about to charge a matador whose back was turned. But the black-suited figure didn't so much as twitch a finger.

Okay, dude. Fair warning, fairly given.

She could clearly see the path she'd have to take, tracing it with an artist's spatial accuracy in her mind's eye. About a hundred yards to build speed straight towards him, half a second to swerve away and miss creaming the creepy fucker, fifty feet or so out onto the soft shoulder, another fifty yards back to the road.

And a few hundred miles to the border without stopping for gas or to check if he's still behind you.

The battered vehicle roared another warning. She couldn't tell if Agent 97 blinked under those shades, but he certainly didn't move – no sign he was even remotely concerned about being a bloody smear on the highway.

Oh, well. Here goes.

Zara jammed the gearshift into *drive* and pounding the gas in the same instant. The car dove forward, tires screaming, the bull eager for the feel of guts on its face. It devoured the measly hundred yards in a fury of thrown gravel, the engine coughing its protest but still plowing forward. Inches from the toes of Agent 97's wingtips, Zara pulled the handbrake like she'd seen in so many car chases. The car lurched sideways, and she released the brake, hauling on the steering wheel with everything she had and clearing the man in black just as she'd planned. She imagined she could see his pores as she whizzed past the SUV and onto the shoulder.

Which was softer than she'd thought.

The thirsty ground had guzzled the rain of the last two days with porn-starlet gusto, turning what should've been a tractionable chunk of ground into sticky mire. Balding tires bit into the mud and sank almost immediately, spinning furiously and flinging sludge.

"Fuck! No, no, no, come on! Don't do this to me, you shit-smoking fuckface!" Zara howled. She pumped the gas pedal and rocked back and forth in her seat, trying to will the ton of rust to do her bidding.

But the poor, abused machine had given up the fight. The engine rumbled to a pitiful, squelching stop as the undercarriage clogged with mud. It had been an exciting day for the little car – much more fun than shuttling around its original broski driver – but it had been totally used up. With a final, heroic shudder, the beater ended its life as a getaway car and headed to the big junkyard in the sky.

Cock, Zara thought, her shaking hands gripping the steering wheel like a passenger on the *Titanic* would a piece of floating debris. *Now what?*

She glanced up into the rearview mirror and saw... nothing.

There was the black SUV looming a few dozen feet behind her but no sign of Agent 97. Every hair on her body rose to attention, and all the hot excitement from the chase evaporated and allowed a trickle of icy fear take its place. She scanned around, looking for any sign of him.

Windshield – nothing.

Passenger side – nothing.

Rear window – nothing.

Driver's side - ...

Snick.

She didn't have time to think as her seatbelt was cut away. Black-gloved hands grabbed her narrow shoulders, dragging her effortlessly through the open driver's side window. One second she'd been trying to pick out a human figure in the trees; the next, her knees were slamming against concrete as she was hauled by the armpits towards the black SUV.

"Miss Zara Carter, I am taking you into protective custody," Agent 97 said flatly as he frog-marched her to his car. "You have no official rights in this circumstance, and as such, I will not read you any. I will be transporting you from this location whether or not you agree to be transported." His iron hold didn't waver, despite Zara's energetic twisting and attempts to bite his arms. "If you continue to resist, I am authorized to use any means necessary to ensure your cooperation. You will arrive at the holding facility alive and intact but possibly unconscious." The droning voice would've fooled anyone listening. He wasn't forcibly detaining a squirming, wild girl with one hand; he was reading the quarterly report to a roomful of bureaucrats.

Despite Zara's vigorous efforts to escape, Agent 97 covered the intervening distance to his vehicle with robotic efficiency. His left hand opened the back passenger door, and his right pressed down on Zara's shoulder, urging her to climb into the seat without more protests.

Yeah, right.

She pushed back with her remaining strength, bracing herself against the door frame, and propping one foot against the runner for leverage. But she hardly budged. Agent 97 shifted his grip with lightning speed, sliding his detaining hand from her arm and closing it around the back of her neck, pressing her forward. Zara grunted and screwed up her face with the effort of resisting, sweat pouring off her; he merely stood his ground, face stoic. They locked that way – Zara fighting to break free, Agent 97 simply holding her where she was.

It only took a few seconds for Zara to wish she'd lifted more weights. Muscles quivered and bones creaked with the effort of resistance. *We can't hold out much longer, Captain!* She willed her joints to lock in place. She silently prayed to whatever god would listen. But it was no use – her body gave up, and she plunged into the SUV's rear bench seat, a tangle of bloodless limbs.

She sprawled face down against the cool leather on the verge of bursting into tears, her anger and energy spent. She heard a *thud* behind her and waited for the engine to start. Waited for Agent 97 to take her to her doom.

And waited.

And waited.

Morbidly curious that nothing had happened, Zara risked a glance over her shoulder.

Standing in the open doorway where the imposingly-cut figure of her jailer should have been was a shortish, roundish, girlish silhouette, holding what looked like a twisted stop sign.

"Looks like I got here just in time," the shadow said, stepping into the pool of yellow light cast by the open car door.

It was Sofi.

She grinned at Zara, proudly waving the steel road sign as if it were a twig. She straddled the limp body of Agent 97, who appeared to be unrumpled even when sprawled unconscious in the middle of the highway.

"You coming or what?" asked Sofi. She offered her hand to Zara.

After a long moment to untangle herself – arms and legs were still rubbery after the battle of wills – Zara tumbled out of the SUV and landed heavily in Sofi's strong arms. The tickle-torture of blood recirculating in her extremities precluded all attempts at standing under her own power. Leaning on Sofi for support until the spiky urchins retreated, she looked over the body of her pursuer.

"He's not...dead. Is he?" she asked apprehensively.

"Nah," Sofi said. She chucked the ruined stop sign into the gloom with one hand, still supporting Zara with the other. It flew a good forty feet before it landed with a soft *pomf*. "I only whanged him hard enough to knock him out. But he'll have the mother of all headaches when he wakes up." She peered closer at the back of Agent 97's head; a palm-length mat of bloody hair had formed there. "And maybe an interesting story to tell the ER nurse."

"What do we do with him?" Zara asked. She nudged his arm with the toe of her boot. "He'll be pissed when he wakes up, and he won't stop looking for me just 'cause he's got a headache. Seems sort of single-minded like that."

Sofi pursed her lips as she thought, one of her few surviving girly habits. "I hadn't really planned that far ahead, to be honest. I just figured I'd catch up with you down the road, not have to assault a federal agent and rescue a damsel in distress."

Zara blushed slightly.

A tiny thought tugged at her sleeve. "Wait a minute," she said. "Where the hell were you, anyway? I waited for half an hour at the gas station."

Sofi pointed back towards town. "I took a detour after seeing a couple SUVs blocking the usual exits. One of them followed me for a while, so I had to duck down alleys a couple of times and hide in a parking garage once. Turns out all our runs gave me a great map of the best places to hide.

"When I got this far, I saw two vehicles at the top of the ridge, and I figured it was probably a bad sign. Picked up the stop sign about halfway up here, just in case."

Sofi had started walking back in the direction of her car as she was talking but stopped short as if she'd remembered something. Zara narrowly avoided plowing into her as she turned around.

"Got an idea," Sofi said. "Go grab your backpack out of your car while I take care of this guy."

Hustling back to Agent 97's prone form, she patted him down and rummaged through a few pockets. Three peppermints; a travel-sized floss dispenser; an extremely expensive-looking pen; a small notebook bound with rubber bands; an all-black credit card with no brand; not a scrap of pocket lint or used Kleenex, and notably, no ID.

Most boring secret agent ever.

After a few minutes of searching, she turned up a set of keys, which she held jingled triumphantly at Zara as the other girl rejoined her.

"I know it won't stop him, but it'll at least slow him down," she explained as she slid them into her jeans pocket. "I wonder if men in black have Triple A?"

As they walked to the getaway car, Sofi pressed a button on her own keychain and its engine rumbled to life. The vehicle's headlights switched on automatically and bathed everything in a soft LED light.

Zara's breath caught. She didn't know shit about cars, but she couldn't help being impressed as she ran her fingers over the hood. Eric had never shown anyone what was under the dustcover in the garage side of his workshop. It was obviously a vehicle, but he kept insisting it wasn't done yet and refused to talk about it until it was. Rumors of the contents included: stripped-down muscle car, stolen mini-tank, souped-up trike, and secret alien spacecraft. Turned out the first camp had it right. The midnight-black body's sleek lines and engine's sonorous rumble stirred up thoughts in Zara inappropriate for an inanimate object. Bleeding-edge tech that must've taken Eric months to acquire glittered in the dash, blue light bouncing off the leather interior.

"He *gave* this to you?" Zara breathed.

Sofi dropped into the driver's seat. "I know, right? Thing's a monster." Then added with a grin, "A sexy, sexy monster."

She patted the seat beside her. "C'mon, Z, we gotta go. There'll be plenty of time for molesting the car later."

Zara grinned lopsidedly and tossed her backpack into the back seat. She slid neatly into the passenger side, enjoying the sensation of heated leather on her aching muscles.

Damn but he did a great job with this thing. Can't believe he just gave it to us after all those years of work. Too bad I won't get to thank him for it...

Her heart sank a bit. She hated making herself sad like that.

The night out here was so different from the kind you got in the city. In Steeltown, all you had was the simple absence of sunlight to let you know it might be time to go to bed (or start prowling, depending on your line of work). The night there crackled with electricity and neon, never really resting, only muted and on pause; everything biding its time until the next sunup. But once you broke free of the streetlights, stoplights, headlights, and nightlights, there was nothing to muddy the black-black of the sky, nothing to pollute the sparkle of the stars. Out here, there was real rest.

The window Zara looked out of seemed proud to be displaying the cream-colored full moon as it gazed down over the valley's pine forests and rocky foothills. She felt as if the sky itself wanted to envelop her in its velvet blanket and whisk her away from all the madness chasing her.

If only it was that easy.

She nearly leapt out of her skin as her reverie shattered. Sofi had reached over and silently put a tiny hand on Zara's knobby knee, squeezing it slightly for reassurance. Once the terror subsided, Zara's heart momentarily swelled with gratitude for her friend, for everything she'd given up to make sure she was safe. Ignoring the protests of her heart's vehement guardian, she took Sofi's hand and squeezed back.

Everything was going to be okay.

Agent 97 stared at the pavement through his shatter-proof sunglasses. He'd lain there for a long time, conscious but not stirring, taking a careful physical inventory before allowing himself to move.

Legs/feet/toes: intact.

Arms/hands/fingers: intact.

Head/neck/brain: moderate abrading to skull, possible concussion.

Internal bleeding: none.

Verdict: alive, largely unharmed, approved for mobility.

He pried himself off the filthy road in push-up stance and leapt cleanly to his feet like an Olympic gymnast. Brushing debris from his suit, he made a cursory survey of the area.

Time: 2214. Approximately seven hours until sunrise. No sign of assailant. Subject has eluded capture but vehicle is inoperable. Own vehicle still present. Evidence of unidentified vehicle proceeding past authorized roadblock. Possible person of interest and potential accessory. Pursue and capture.

Confident in his findings as always, Agent 97 moved to the driver's side of his vehicle and reached into a crisply starched pocket for the keys.

He frowned.

He searched another pocket. His brow creased.

Another pocket. Nothing.

His hands methodically inspected his perfectly-tailored attire for his car keys. Finding nothing, he executed a precise sweep of the ten square meters around his person and the subject's vehicle. Still nothing.

As a rule, Agent 97 didn't get perplexed or annoyed; such debilitating emotions had been systematically trained out of him as a young recruit. Yet this situation caused him a measure of mental discomfort, a phantom of irritation haunting him for his laxity. It flickered across his brain which immediately flashed a neon-red *rejected* sign.

Quickly, as if to make up for the momentary lack of reason, his mind performed the calculations for potential scenarios in which his keys could have disappeared. Scenario 07 yielded the most likely situation: stolen by subject (92.7% probability).

He didn't sigh with frustration. He didn't curse the subject and accomplice. He didn't even roll his eyes skyward in annoyance. What he did do was fish out one of the peppermints, pop it in his mouth, and take up an at-ease stance on the side of the road. There, he waited patiently, knowing the department had already received the distress signal from his subdermal vital signs monitor. A helicopter would arrive in approximately an hour and thirty-three minutes to retrieve him.

And then he could resume the hunt.

It was nearly two in the morning before either of the girls spoke again. Their familiar pattern of intimate silence tucked itself between and around them like a security blanket. The whir of tires on the asphalt was hypnotic, and Sofi had started to doze off, so Zara had taken the wheel when they stopped for gas. It only took a few more miles for both of them to acknowledge they needed to stop for the night, lest they end up on the news as *Teen Girls Die in Fiery Car Wreck*.

"Where do we go, though?" Sofi asked. "It's not like we can check into a motel. There's probably dudes crawling all over this area looking for us."

As if by way of a cosmic answer, a huge brown road sign came into the headlights.

Mountain Cave National Park: Next Exit.

"Good enough for me," Zara said.

The gravel road past the dark ranger's station gave the hot rod a bit of nose-scraping trouble, but a clearing a few yards off the camper's path made a perfect hiding spot. Zara, her crime novel radar going berserk, managed to convince Sofi to cover their too-magnificent car with fallen pine branches before they set off looking for a convenient cave to spend the night in. Even if there was a trail of flattened scrub behind them, they had to cover as many tracks as possible.

The woods here showed all the signs of preparing for winter, including a bone-chilling wind that cut straight through the girls' autumn city jackets. Their feet sank easily into a loamy bed of dead leaves, pine needles, and wet soil as they trudged up towards the mountainside. Flighty, naked deciduous trees stood awkwardly silhouetted between their fully-clothed evergreen cousins like freshmen at a senior prom. The musky, macerating scent of the dying forest filled the air with thoughts of hibernation. Sticker bushes with their hooked fingers tried weakly to hold Zara as she walked past. Sofi's flashlight picked out small rocks peeking out of the ground, waiting to trip inattentive passerby, which soon gave way to stately boulders as they climbed.

"There's one," Sofi said, pointing off to the right.

A narrow cavity in the stone edifice was outlined in the moonlight a few steps from where they stood. Sofi pushed on ahead and inspected the cave. No good finding out it's a gang hangout after you've fallen asleep, after all. The place was dry and fairly shallow, had a low ceiling, as out of the wind, and came furnished with a handful of comfortable-looking rocks. Seemed okay to her.

She poked her head back out and gave Zara a thumbs-up.

"Welcome to the Rock Motel," she said, waving her arms expansively. "Wake up is at whenever you can't stand sleeping on the floor anymore, and breakfast is whatever you can forage without poisoning yourself."

Zara snorted appreciatively, and Sofi threw her backpack down next to a flat stone. She propped the flashlight up against it and cranked the brightness down so the glow couldn't be seen from outside. Rummaging in the pack a bit, she retrieved a couple of slightly-smashed PB&J sandwiches and offered one to Zara who was using her own bag as a butt cushion.

"I think we can avoid the whole poisoning thing," she said. "At least until we cross the border. Never know what foreign food will do to you."

Zara took the sandwich and merrily tucked in as if there would never be another one. Grape jam was her favorite. She was glad Sofi had thought to bring real food; that had been the last thing on her mind when she stormed off, and all she'd brought was a clutch of now-crushed Twinkies.

Sofi watched intently as the other girl unwrapped the tinfoil, her eyes on the alert for any signs of... well, she wasn't sure exactly. Anything weird. But rather than being melancholy like Sofi expected, Zara seemed more alive than ever. The action-movie escape and secret hideout lit up that dark face in ways she had only seen on adrenaline highs. She smiled to herself as she remembered those first magical days when the inkpen had brought Zara such joy, even if it was only temporary.

Which reminded her...

"Hey, Z."

"Ymsh?" Zara said through a mouthful of peanut butter.

"I brought you something. Forgot about it until just now."

She felt around in the recesses of her bag until her fingers hit what she was looking for: a small, hand-carved box. Wordlessly, she held it out.

Zara swallowed the last of her sandwich and took the box in both hands. She ran her fingers gingerly over the tangle of full-bloom roses and stylized briars that decorated the lid. Her skin tingled; she wasn't sure if it was the thought of Eric, now left behind, or the call of the inkpen nesting insides. She could feel the device through the thick wood, sweetly keening for her touch and fully expecting her to reach in and reunite them.

"Why'd you bring it?" she asked softly. "I left it behind on purpose. I didn't want it to wind up in Azkaban with me."

"I know, but if it gives you even a little happiness, I thought you should have it."

She knew Sofi was right. She could feel the lock on her heart creaking with anticipation as she held the instrument in its box. Even being away from the inkpen for a few hours, the darkness inside her had intensified; it had gotten a taste of the light, and now it was hooked like a toddler drinking a Coke. She'd tried for so long to appease her inner guardian and failed every time. Nothing she could find, be, do, or say was enough to make him unlock the doors. If he wouldn't let her break the chains for good, it seemed like the fleeting elation of impressing art into flesh was her only option.

A few stolen moments are better than nothing at all, right?

She sniffed a little, trying to corral the tears threatening to jump from her eyelashes, and her voice only croaked slightly when she spoke.

"Thanks, Soph. Really." She gave a thin, watery smile.

Sofi leaned over abruptly and grabbed Zara into a bear hug. "I just want you to be happy, Z. And I'll go with you wherever you need to go to find that," she whispered, her own voice thick with unspent emotion.

Zara did her best to hug back. "I know."

"Good," said Sofi, letting go, her voice getting back to business. "Now, I think we need to get some sleep. Secret Agent 69 or whatever is probably conscious by now. Let's make sure he doesn't catch up."

She retrieved a small pile of clothes and thin bedding from their backpacks, and they both hunkered down on the chilly stone floor. With only a few hours until dawn, every minute of rest would count, and they still had a long way to go before they could even think about breathing easier.

As she drifted off, Zara wondered if it was even possible to elude Agent 97 with all his high-tech equipment and not-quite-human skillset. But she couldn't answer. Only morning knew for sure.

Sometime during the night, Zara tried to roll over but couldn't. She immediately panicked, visions of straightjackets and padded rooms spinning in her brain. Reaching down, she found that Sofi had wrapped an arm around her waist in her sleep. Zara's hackles dropped, and she smiled a little. She lay back down feeling safer in that flimsy embrace than she had in years behind brick walls and locked doors.

It's so cold I think I'm still awake. I couldn't possibly be so cold and sleeping. I wonder why Sofi isn't keeping me warm.
But Sofi isn't here. I'm alone in this darkness. Like always.

I open my eyes, then I'm not sure I've done it. This is the real dark. The kind you only get underground or underwater. It's so heavy it can't live in the air above.

Eventually, I stand, every limb aching with the frost that crackles along my skin. I feel it crack and fall off as I rise. I've got to go... somewhere. The hazy recollection of a destination floats back to me.

Suddenly, I'm frantic to get there. I whip my head around, looking for any sign of light to guide me, and I start to panic, my sluggish mind catching up to the terror of the situation.

Just as I'm about to scream out in the desperate hope that someone will rescue me, I hear it. A heartbeat. Low and slow, like a dinosaur swallowed me. It comes from everywhere at once, but if I listen hard, really listen, it's ... that way.

I follow the sound, shuffling my feet and holding my hands out for balance. The vibration in my bones grows faintly louder and slightly faster with each step, like the dinosaur is slowly waking up. Like he's excited I'm coming.

The faintest of lights breaks around the next corner like too-ripe raspberries in a bowl of tangerines. I'm so accustomed to the darkness that even this pinprick glow burns. But the heartbeat is faster now, driving and insistent. I rub my eyes until they adjust.

I step across some invisible threshold and here is the source. Heartbeat and light in one shining, impossible object. Its tangled fingers and arms are burning merrily, wrapped around a massive, pink-ice crystal heart locked inside. The heart beats furiously, trying to break through its own frost and revel in the fire, but it can't. Not on its own.

The pounding rhythm grows to deafening pitch, enticing me to come nearer. Fear freezes me to the floor. It thudthudthuds like a peyote-tripping drummer. Harder, faster. Demanding, begging.

Set me free.

Thudthudthud.

I reach out a trembling hand, fingertips brushing the black prison.

Thudthudthud.

Help me.

And then it's morning, and I'm awake, and Sofi is spooning me.

But the thudthudthud is still here. It's real.

It's outside.

The thin light of almost-morning trickled in through Zara's cracked eyelids as she tried to locate the sound. It resonated in her chest, and at first, she'd thought Sofi was snoring. (She was, but in a fine soprano pitch.) *Thud-thud-thud,* a marathoner's heartbeat in the last hundred yards. Disoriented from hours of bone-cracking sleep on the cave floor, she tottered to her feet and peered out the fissure in the mountainside.

Nothing. There wasn't a damn thing out there that she could see. But the sound was louder than ever, so she looked skyward.

Oh. My. God.

"Sofi, wake up!" Zara shouted as she sprinted to the makeshift bunk. Her terror crammed the stony space with echoes and urgency. "Sofi, they found us! There's a motherfucking helicopter circling the park!"

"Huh?" Sofi mumbled, rubbing her sleep-filled eyes with a dirty hand. "Whuz goin' on?" She'd always been a heavy sleeper, and trying to wake her was like trying to raise a zombie without the Necronomicon. You could do it, but you had to use the right words.

Zara shook her by the shoulders, eyes shining with the fear of a furry creature cornered by something with more teeth than brain cells. "Agent 97 found us!" she shouted into Sofi's bleary face.

"Thazz nice."

"No! No, it's not – Sofi, wake up, goddamit! The feds are going to be pouring into this place any second now. What do we do? Help me!"

That did it.

Sofi's eyes cleared instantly. "Where are they? How did they find us?" she asked, suddenly alert.

"I don't know," Zara wailed. "But they've got to be close."

"Let me go take a look."

Zara nodded and wrung her hands as Sofi shrugged on a green sweatshirt and walked cautiously out into the dawn-lit forest.

Although she looked at Zara like a sister, there were some things about her past that Sofi had never brought up, primarily because she was ashamed at running away from a life most kids would smother kittens for. Long family camping trips to the mountains was one of those things. The paunchy, bespectacled Mr. Strella fancied himself a bit of a survivalist, despite being the very essence of an accountant. From the instant they pulled into camp, he'd try to teach her about wilderness safety. She'd dutifully stand there in her sturdy pink hiking boots and weatherproof jacket rolling her eyes while he'd lectured her about tracking, foraging, or shelter-building. He'd prattled on about leaf patterns and trace signs and bird song and a million other things she'd tried to tune out to protect herself from dying of boredom. As a born and bred city kid, she'd never imagined that any of that shit would come in handy, but here she was.

Thanks, Dad.

She stuck to the pine trees to hide her profile from the chopper and did her best to tune out its pervasive whine so she could hear the frequency of the forest. Agonizing minutes passed as she slithered her way down to the camouflaged car, only breaking the occasional twig underfoot. The vantage point let her see all the way to the ranger's station in the thin daylight. She silently cursed herself for not being more vigilant about their parking; it would be all too easy for someone with double-secret spy training to spot them from there. But, she noted, there was zero sign of black government cars, and the birds were all singing, a sure indicator that no predators were around.

Yet.

She hurried back to the cave as quickly as she could without drawing undue attention. When she walked in, Zara was sitting on the ground with the carved inkpen box in her hands, rocking slightly. Sofi had to admit she looked a little crazy.

"So, it looks like we're clear for the time being," she reported in her calmest, most matter-of-fact voice. "I don't see any anyone else out there, and I'm pretty sure the chopper hasn't spotted the car." Zara perked up slightly, and Sofi raised her hands. "It could just be a scout, but there's no way to know how much time we've got."

Zara's face collapsed like a condemned building. Another fat, hot tear slid down to her chin before dripping onto the lid of the box.

"Oh, sweetie," crooned Sofi. She sat down next to her friend and draped an arm around her shoulders. "We'll get out of here. We just have to be careful, that's all."

Zara shook her head violently, her hunted eyes locked on something invisible in the distance. "No, we won't," she burbled. "He's coming, and we won't be able to trick him again. He's going to catch me and take me away and lock me in a padded cell and dissect me and I'll never see you again and I'll never be with Eric and I'll never be happy and I'll never be a real person. Never, never, never."

An involuntary sob choked off her terrified ramble, and she buried her head in Sofi's shoulder.

Rub her back, give her a squeeze or two, make soothing noises.

That was all Sofi's brain could come up with. She tried to force it to do something more productive. Make a plan to escape, say something motivating - anything to not have to sit here and witness Zara unraveling. But nothing came.

Because she's right. The choppers are out there, and Agent 97 isn't dead. They'll be here soon. Not enough time to get her away while she's like this. Not when she's given up.

There's nothing you can do to save her. You failed.

The bile of the denouncement stung Sofi's throat as it choked her, the anxiety forcing tears into her eyes. She could feel her tattoo itch as the flush of shame burned its way down her body.

Some momma bear you turned out to be.

She renewed her grip on Zara as if she could save her by holding on tightly enough.

They sat that way for several minutes as Zara sobbed into Sofi's armpit and Sofi fought against falling into her own pit of despair.

Her mind whirred without gaining traction, every second that passed another nail in their coffin. The sound of the chopper was getting consistently louder as it narrowed its search radius. Sofi figured they had two hours, maybe. Enough time for the scout to report back and mobilize the cavalry, then have that wannabe-Matrix fucker waltz in to kidnap Zara and take her to freak prison.

Zara stirred. "Why is this happening, Sofi? All I ever did with that stupid inkpen was make people happy," she sniffed, her ragged voice muffled by a layer of sweater. She raised bloodshot eyes to meet

Sofi's gaze. "All I ever wanted was to feel something besides fear or guilt or numbness. Why do these assholes want to stick me in a room with no windows for that?" Her brow furrowed as she was overcome by a fresh wave of desperate grief.

Something clicked softly into place inside Sofi's mind. Something so simple she hadn't thought of it before.

"Z..." Her voice was barely a whisper, as if speaking the words would make what she was about to suggest impossible. "I know you said you were afraid to do it before, but..." She trailed off, unsure of how to continue without bursting into tears.

But it's not like anything could be worse than this, right?

The *thudthudthud* of the helicopter's flight was a constant now, providing an ominous soundtrack that filled up the silence between them as Zara searched Sofi's face.

Her eyes widened. Her breathing steadied. Her tears stopped.

Both of them looked down to the engraved box sitting in Zara's lap.

"I told you, I don't know what'll happen," Zara said tentatively.

"I know, but what if it works? What if it gives you everything you wanted, even if it's just for a few minutes?"

Zara chewed her bottom lip as she turned the idea over in her mind. She could see the fork in the road paved by anyone but her, like it had been most of her life. But now she had a choice; the future was hers to decide for the first time since she'd run away. Going down one path, she went with Agent 97 without ever knowing if the inkpen could give her what she needed most. Going down the other, she put the needle to her own skin and trusted herself to fate. But what would fate decide?

"What if…" she started, but she couldn't bring herself to finish the sentence. She could see in Sofi's eyes that she didn't need to say it.

Sofi put her hand over Zara's and squeezed gently. "I'm right here."

The artist nodded, her jaw now set with determination. No matter what happened, at least she would know that she chose how it would end.

Someone at the Supernatural Cases Department had completely overreacted. Most likely Agent 63. He was technically the senior officer, but only by a fluke of chronology; nearly seventy years old, he'd been a field agent the longest, but his middling rank made him junior to fresh-faced young men he could've sired. Word around the building was the he'd been demoted from 99 to 40 when he was in his fifties for tampering with evidence. Most likely, he'd lifted unicorn horn for "personal use." After that, Agent 63 had to claw his way back up the food chain, which had turned him into a pompous ass, even by bureaucratic standards. Calling in air support, emergency medical services, and half a dozen undercover squad cars for one unconscious agent was definitely his handiwork.

Agent 97 preferred a more delicate approach. He'd had plenty of time to think under the washed-out light of vehicles while EMS swabbed, ointmented, and bandaged the stop sign gash in the back of his skull. They'd run him through a battery of mental competence exams that a child would have found tedious.

What is your given name? Agent 97.

What color is the sky? Black.

Who is the current president? That's classified.

As they ticked each official box as he passed their tests, his mind tabulated the new case data in the background.

One subject, one assailant. Headed north-north-west in a modified performance vehicle. Assuming at least one forced stop to refuel to 100% capacity, and factoring in the current time and the time of the attack, the suspects are most likely within the vicinity of Mountain Cave State Park. The terrain in that area is primarily pine forest and is closed to visitors at this time of year. Subjects are most likely physically exhausted and will have stopped to rest before continuing to travel.

He checked the display screen of a watch-like device strapped to his wrist. The tech was practically antique, but Agent 97 refused to be distracted by the newest shiny objects, and he stuck with what worked. The miniature screen of the tracker showed him a flashing blue dot on a grid. At least not all of his training had failed him.

Superlative.

"What is the square root of negative -- "

"The answer is *i*," Agent 97 cut in, holding up an imperious gloved hand. "Thank you for your assistance, but it is no longer required. I am clearly of both sound mind and body, and you are hindering me in my inquiries. I require that we end these tests and immediately resume the pursuit of the subject."

The EMS worker blinked at him a few times but didn't offer any resistance. She obediently stepped aside and let Agent 97 stride from the back of the ambulance and into the darkness. The insistent pulsing of circling helicopter blades and the glare of vehicle headlights nearby made his exit ten percent more dramatic than Agent 97 found appropriate.

Protocol demanded that any lone agent damaged during an active case was to be immediately accompanied by two lower-ranking agents for the remainder of the pursuit. The rule was designed for the protection of high-value agents and also served as a convenient training method for the younger officers. Its enactment was extremely rare and embarrassing to any agent over 50. For it to happen to Agent 97 was devastating; there was a near-60% chance he'd return to his office and find a different man sitting there, his own meager belongings shunted to a below-70 cubicle.

But he wasn't thinking about that now.

Agent 97 addressed his questionable honor guard as he marched across the still-closed highway. "Agent 11. Agent 14. I see you have been assigned to this case. Very good. Your work thus far has been commendable, and I fully expect it to continue to be so."

The two young officers, who had been leaning against their SUV and swapping dirty jokes, snapped smartly to attention as if shocked in a sensitive place with a cattle prod. They'd heard about Agent 97 – the mayor of Don't Fuck Around Town – and they fully intended to avoid fucking around. At least until he was well out of sight.

Agent 97 stiffly nodded his approval at their manners. Most new SCD agents were prepubescent boys who had seen too many spy films, and he found it severely detrimental to the department. He needed straight-minded, uncomplicated men, not children who couldn't tell reality from fantasy. That sort of erroneous judgment killed agents. If he could impress upon these rookies the importance of seriousness and care in ones' work, all the better for the department.

"We will be tracking two subjects into Mountain Cave National Park, approximately two hundred miles from this location," he intoned, hands clasped behind his back. "They have been hiding there overnight as a resting place before they continue their flight. We will make quick progress to the site with the assistance of a helicopter scout and cleared roadways. It is currently oh-four-seventeen; we will be arriving in the park at approximately oh-seven-fifty-five. Once we have arrived, the two of you will stay with the vehicles to block any direct escape route. Wait for me there until you are instructed otherwise. A tracking device has been planted on the primary subject during a physical confrontation, and relevant information updates will be disseminated should circumstances change. The helicopter will provide aerial support in the unlikely event that the initial capture attempt fails. My role will be to penetrate the forest and retrieve the suspects."

A muffled snort came from one of the agents.

"Do you find something humorous in this briefing, Agent 11?"

The red-haired officer readjusted his at-attention stance, suddenly all seriousness and respect. "No, sir."

Agent 97's eyes narrowed slightly behind his opaque sunglasses, and suddenly he was an inch from Agent 11's freckled nose. "That is most wise, Agent 11. You will find that this department does not tolerate the childish games you seem predisposed to. I strenuously suggest you reevaluate your commitment to your position and eradicate such puerile behavior. It makes you a weak and vulnerable target for the forces with which we interact each day. It would be a moderate drain on department resources to replace you, should you find yourself the main course at a faerie feast."

Agent 11's eyes had grown wider and wider as he was dressed down, and Agent 97 noted with disgust that they'd become shiny with tears.

Soft. Fanciful. Imaginative. Weak.

He held the younger man's gaze for a long moment to press his point home, then stepped back and said, "You have your orders. Move out."

The boys practically fled into the safety of their vehicle.

It was 0754 when the black SUVs crunched into the gravel parking lot in front of the visitor center. The spare minute grated on Agent 97, and he remained seated and buckled in his vehicle until it passed. Punctuality was vital to the success of a mission, and arriving early was worse than arriving late. His predecessor had been killed in the line of duty when he surprised a banshee forty-five seconds too soon.

When he finally did alight from the car, he didn't speak to Agents 11 and 14. They needed to learn independence and responsibility, and his assistance would only hinder their already-stunted progress towards that goal. He smoothed the sleeves of his suit jacket and brushed microscopic flecks of dirt from the lapels. He nodded curtly once to the younger agents to remind them of their role, then started up the hill towards the cave where the corresponding blue dot on his tracker was hiding.

Sofi knew there was someone in the woods even before she heard the rustle of the leaves. The chopper had broken off its vigil a few minutes ago, and the forest had fallen deathly silent, the birds holding their breath as they waited for the predator to pass. The faint whiff of cologne drifted to her on the breeze under the heavy autumn scent of rotting foliage and damp moss. She'd have to be quick.

Trying not to crunch too many brown pine needles, she tiptoed between fallen branches and half-buried stones looking for a suitable place to bury the damn thing. Her tear-blurred vision made the terrain more dangerous than it had been in the dark, and the box shook in her trembling hands, but she pressed on. It was a huge risk coming out here, and she knew it. Almost anyone could've spotted her now that the sun was up, even with her dad's pseudo-training to help her. She should've been back in the cave, protecting Zara. But she didn't have a choice: the inkpen couldn't fall into the wrong hands. Agent 97 definitely had the wrong hands.

The stink of aftershave was getting stronger, trilling on some animal instinct that made Sofi desperate to chuck the box into the woods, hope for the best, and sprint back to the cave. She wasn't sure if he was three feet or a hundred yards away; the bear paw tattoo had come with strange senses, and she still hadn't entirely calibrated to them. Glancing over her shoulder, she couldn't see anyone, but the fear that he might get to Zara before she did overthrew caution.

Fuck it.

She dropped to her knees and pulled up the forest's winter blanket of grass, moss, and leaves with both hands, piling the earth next to the hole. A fingernail bent back and snapped off, but she didn't stop. No time. All she could think of was that spooky motherfucker slinking into the cave and hauling Zara away to some top-secret building with no windows.

The fear and fury pushed her on blindly until she hit a gnarly, ancient tree root, sacrificing another nail. Growling under her breath, she shoved the box into the hole and slung the pile of debris back on top of it. She maintained presence of mind long enough to arrange the topsoil so it looked relatively undisturbed, then she bolted back down the hill, back to the cave, back to Zara.

If he could hear her, it was a safe assumption that she could hear him. These particular subjects demonstrated supernaturally acute senses, and it would be grievously unwise to underestimate their abilities. The wrist tracker showed that his primary quarry was likely concealed in one of the park's many caverns, approximately 26 meters north-northwest of his current location. Why the other subject had ventured into the forest would have to be determined later. By his best calculations, he had approximately three minutes to reach their hiding place before she returned.

Not that he had any concern whatsoever about facing them as a pair, he told himself. It would simply be easier to deal with them one at a time.

He pushed on, attempting to silence his passage as best he could, which wasn't much. The vast majority of underage anomaly cases happened in urban settings, and SCD training spent a mere day on outdoor survival skills. Leaves and branches littered the forest floor, concealing ankle-twisting stones and rightfully angry rodents, all of them making it obvious to anyone in a kilometer radius that someone was approaching. Twice he paused to listen for the girl in the woods, but she seemed to have gone. This unsettled Agent 97 and gave him a brief post-traumatic flashback to his first bloody encounter with a lycanthrope.

This event bears no resemblance to that case. Neither of the current subjects exhibit level eight abilities; they are a significantly reduced risk. Continue the pursuit or you will lose them again.

Sixteen meters and closing. You have two minutes.

Half-running, half-leaf-surfing, Sofi made it back to the cave just in time. The aftershave smell had been so strong when she'd walked in that she was afraid it was too late. But there was no sign of Agent Smith or whatever his name was. More bear-sense tricks.

Now, though, there was nothing to do but wait. No use trying to make a run for it with the net closing so quickly and so tight. Nowhere in here to hide, either. Sofi gathered the contents of her backpack, carefully folding and tucking each item away, then moved to sit beside Zara, holding the oversized bag in front of her like a blockade. She rested her head on the soft bundle and squeezed her eyes shut.

If I can't see you, then you can't see me, right?

Yeah, right. He can't avoid seeing this, even if he wanted to.

She listened to the agent's halting progress outside, his shuffling footsteps closing nearer and nearer. She waited. She cried a little.

And she avoided Zara. The tattoo had changed her friend too much, and Sofi couldn't bring herself to look at the terrible, magnificent work of art she'd created. It only made her heart stop beating and her breath dissolve and her tears start again.

The click of city shoes on rough stone.

A figure outlined against the morning sunshine.

Day-old cologne.

Agent 97 wordlessly crossed the threshold of the cave and stood in front of the disheveled girl clutching a leather backpack. The never-resting calculator in his mind studied her face and pulled up her mental file.

Sofi Strella, age 20. 90.5% likelihood of wielding the stop sign responsible for my injuries. Possibly highly dangerous even unarmed. Do not engage unless attacked.

Sofi raised her eyes defiantly from his mud-ruined shoes to the impenetrable black sunglasses. Every inch of her wanted to lash out, to finish the job she'd started out there on the highway. To dig into his skin with nails and teeth and feel his blood running down her elbows. But she knew it wouldn't change anything, and she stayed put.

"This is all your fault," she hissed from between clenched teeth, spitting the syllables like poison darts. The cave walls echoed the last word a few times before letting it evaporate.

Agent 97 ignored her accusation and looked down at the prone figure beside her.

He took a half step forward, then hesitated.

His ever-stony face cracked as he raised one eyebrow in surprise.

Slowly, carefully, he removed his sunglasses.

The instant I touch the cool metal of the inkpen, lightning dives into my skin. It punctures every vein simultaneously with cool blue fire, with the sweetest kisses, with the sharpest knives. It's a deluge of the familiar-yet-foreign overload of pleasure. It skims along the edges of my mind and reads my thoughts. It whispers without speaking, its hissing angel's voice rejoicing, doing backflips in anticipation.

Nownownow. Yesyesyes.

I can see the fear in Sofi's eyes as I lift the pen. She trembles with trepidation I can't afford to feel. She holds it for me. All that's left inside my skin is the lightning.

I wonder briefly if I look like the soldiers on the news, the ones radiating resolution and grim purpose. I set my jaw to imitate that courage, hoping to draw in just a little more. Just enough to do what needs to be done.

I waver.

I continue.

My eyes flutter shut – I'm not sure if I close them or if they do it on their own - and the inkpen cranks its electricity. Like a heavy metal drummer discovering a double kick pedal. The pounding of it races my blood so fast I'm afraid my skin will burn and peel from the carnal-heat redness of my bare skin.

No mirror, not even the strange reflected light of the cavern to help me. I don't need it. The design is seared into my fingers by years of drawing the same image over and over and over. Always the same, always different, always something I can't quite touch even though it erupts from the molten core of me. I wake and live it, sleep and dream it. My hands will pour out the meaning; the inkpen will channel it into the living canvas of my flesh. Where it has always belonged and never been.

I press the needle to my chest, just over my heart. My shattered-and-glued-back-together heart. My missing-pieces-and-edges heart. My locked-up-

and-thrown-away-the-key heart. My iceberg-in-the-freezing-ocean heart. It jumps to meet the needle's point. It tries to shatter its bony cage just to kiss the face of its savior.

The shock of contact is over in milliseconds. Nanoseconds. Inverse seconds. No pain. Reverse pain. Taking pain away from memories, as if pain had never happened.

The only evidence that the inkpen has even pricked my skin is the deliciously butter-melting glow that radiates across unending acres of my body. I roll on forever. In the tiny part of my mind capable of thought, I wonder if Sofi can see it. I wonder if I'm as luminous outside as inside.

And now there is nothing but flow.

I conduct a thousand-piece orchestra. I trace the journey of a continental railroad. I author the Great American Novel. I oversee the rise and fall of an empire. I paint the ceiling of the Sistine Chapel. I sketch out the future, the present, the past. I etch my heart onto the outside.

Heart to collarbone. Collarbone to throat. Throat to heart. Simple, sketched lines that expand and curl and shade themselves under the inkpen's *eagerness to cover every inch of blood-flushed skin. A wild and unconstrained tangle of lines, angles, curves, shades, emptiness.*

Red and black. Stems and thorns. Briars and blossoms.

Ink and skin.

The roses unfurl as they're drawn, leaping from buds to tissue-thin petals in an instant, they're so eager to be born. I feel each one open, brushing along my too-hot self like a nearly-missed kiss. Carmine and vermillion. Claret and ruby. Crimson and scarlet. The blossoms spread baby-soft wings, covering the empty spaces between thorns and stems until no gap remains. Every inch of my chest is filled with enormous dewy flowers, each one driving its tangled, black roots straight down, searching for a safe, warm place to connect.

As the last perfect black line flows across the parchment of my skin, the roses' grasping fingers seize the lock on my heart.

The power of the spark forces a gasp from my lips, and the inkpen clatters to the floor. I hear the sound from a zillion miles away; someone miles underwater asks me if I'm okay. I open my mouth to reassure them but the words don't come. The roots wrap themselves around my core, forcing me to be in my body.

All I can do is keep breathing.

I stand before my heart, locked and chained and guarded oh so valiantly. Roots, thorns, and stems rush past, eager to begin the battle.

The guardian of my heart remains stalwart against the invasion. He defends his post to the last, sword and shield slick with black ichor as he sinks to his knees. In his final moment, he salutes me. I nod to acknowledge his bravery, and he slumps to the ground, duty fulfilled. I have fought against him so many times, desperate to break the chains of the post I condemned him to, and alwaysalwaysalways, he would win. But now it's time to open the doors that have been sealed with fear and hate and shame for far too long.

Thorny rose fingers insinuate themselves into the immense lock holding the chains tight around the vault of my heart. I gasp again, this time in pain. Each tumbler clicking into place slams another shock of agony into my chest.

Click – slam – gasp.

Click – slam – gasp.

Click – slam – gasp.

Out in the world, my fingernails bite into the still-fresh ink on my skin, clutching my chest and trying to peel away the roses. My heart pounds furiously with irregular rhythm as it fights against the unlocking. I fear the force of it, as if I'll collapse in on myself like a dying star.

Then, silence.

Stillness.

The ancient chains collapse, the lock disintegrated into dust.

A single thin stem reaches out, grasps the handle, turns, pulls.

The objection of disused hinges fighting rust. The scream of metal bending against its will. The stink of musty air as the doors fall open.

Even the rose roots anxiously hold their breath.

What will emerge from the dusty shadow? A corpse? A child? Nothing at all? What could survive ten years in solitary confinement, a decade in captivity?

A razor-edge of light appears, so tiny it's almost invisible. Every ragged breath I take intensifies the light as it slowly fills up the prison that's been made of my heart. The pool of illumination swells and surges. Dull yellow to bright white. At its peak, I'm blinded; my eyes are so used to the darkness here. But my vision clears, and the captive stands before me, waiting to be recognized.

A rose.

The size and color of a smog-laced sunset.

Unhurt and unblemished by the severity and length of its banishment, it unfolds and unfolds and unfolds until it envelops its former cell, leaving no trace that it had ever been a prisoner.

It beckons to me with a voice like the rustle of leaves against petals.

I can't resist. I step forward automatically, the only possible action. The ruddy light the flower casts leaves everything glowing brighter and stronger with each moment as I meet this queen of roses, slipping easily into her waiting folds.

The heart of my heart.

The love of my love.

The hope of my hope.

Softer than a newborn rabbit's fur. Warmer than the summer ocean. Safer than a hundred locks on a thousand chains. More right than if I had never been wronged.

They'd waited patiently as I communed with my prisoner. But they could wait no longer. Like impatient children rushing to their mother after days apart, the black roots of the roses on my skin race forward, sinking every tendril into their queen.

Into their home.

Into my heart.

Into me.

On the other side of the galaxy, in the place where Sofi watches over me, the impact rocks my frail and unresisting body so hard I sprawl onto the icy floor of the cave. I can hear her, the underwater voice coming to the surface. She lifts me into her lap, babbling incoherently in her fear, checking my pulse and fretting.

I open my eyes and see relief flood her face. I smile up at her, unguarded and unimaginable radiance pouring out of me. I can feel it so clearly. It surges in leaps and bounds from every cell, wanting to share the joy with her. For everything she's done, everything she's meant to me. For being my friend, my partner, my confidant, my critic, my cheerleader. My only family. For years of stony coldness when all I wanted was to love her the way she loves me.

I want to tell her everything. About the roses and the guardian and the opening and the prisoner-queen and how everything is okay.

Because now I can.

Because I am a whole girl.

Because her plan worked.

Sofi smiles back at me, tears streaming down her face and dripping off her chin. She trembles, unable to contain the uproar of emotions that compete for attention inside her. The relief pours off her in swells of laughter. I start to laugh, too.

But something happens. A stirring in my chest, just below the roses.

I sink back, half-lidded and half-electrified, immobilized and waiting for the next wave. What else have I been hiding inside that prison? What more do the roses have in store for me?

I see Sofi's face fall, her eyes wide in disbelief and panic. She desperately screams something I can't hear and clutches me tighter to her. Her nails bite into my shoulders, but it doesn't hurt.

I try to tell her it's okay. As I wet my lips with a sandpaper tongue, my vision dims and Sofi's features soften, then fade.

Back into the darkness.

Agent 97 had worked hundreds of assignments in his tenure at the Supernatural Cases Department. He'd stopped a demon from leaving a changeling in a senator's home. He'd arrested a zombie living behind a Chinese restaurant. He'd stood vigil at the wake of a white wizard as every kind of mythological being came to pay their respects. And because he had so thoroughly trained his mind to see what was really there and nothing else, he had never once been surprised, never been afraid, never even been impressed by what he saw.

But he had never seen anything like this.

Miss Zara Carter, aged 18, orphan, petty criminal, rising artist, and supernatural anomaly, lay on her back in the center of the small cavern, her clothing having been lovingly straightened and her slim hands carefully folded over her navel. Her features were serene, sweetly curling lips and unfurrowed brow suggesting she was on the verge of a smile. A wild halo of black hair pooled around her shoulders. The bare skin of her torso flushed pink. She looked for all the world like she'd simply fallen asleep.

Except for the rose bush growing out of her chest.

Three feet of black stems with tiny yellow thorns tangled around each other, forming a fragile stalk and dozens of thin branches bearing roses so blood-red they should have been dripping. The flowers pulsated in a heartbeat rhythm, emerald green leaves holding them aloft proudly, their petals glittering with dew that had never fallen. The ethereal plant illuminated the simple tribal tattoo that covered Zara's bared chest with a pale pink aura, its sharp-lined briars and soft blooms exactly mirroring the miniature tree that towered over her body. Its home, its host, its mother, its victim.

For the first time since he was a rookie, Agent 97 wasn't sure what to do. He was rooted to the spot, a perfect inverse parallel to his quarry.

And he could feel Sofi's eyes burning into him.

She rose and stood beside him, barely reaching his shoulder but holding herself as if she were a nine-foot tall bear queen. Letting her eyes finally fall on Zara, she kept them trained there. Her voice came out imperious and distant.

"You killed her," she said flatly. A statement of fact more than blame. "All she ever wanted was to feel love and hope and joy - all that emotional bullshit people take for granted. To unlearn what she'd learned from all those years of being fucked over by the world. To be a real person."

Pause. *Sniff.*

"And she was. So slowly I wanted to throttle her, but she was changing. Using that stupid inkpen made her so damn happy. Helping all those people just like her. It was working."

Sofi's voiced cracked and gave out momentarily, steaming tears threatening to ruin her unnerving calm. She turned towards Agent 97 and glared at him as if she could make him explode with her hatred.

"Then you ruined everything."

To her surprise, he turned and met her gaze. Sofi couldn't help noticing his eyes were chocolate brown, just like hers. Without his sunglasses, he looked different somehow. Not intimidating, not threatening. But human. Exposed. Like maybe he wasn't a government spook or a perfectly-programmed robot. Maybe he was just a man doing his job. A man who didn't hate or fear the girl he was chasing. A man covering up sympathy and care to avoid the deep cuts of the world.

In that instant, she could see it as clearly as if he'd said it out loud.

But when she blinked, the fleeting glimpse into his humanity winked out, his naked eyes revealing no more than brown reflections of herself. A sad pear-shaped girl subconsciously flexing iron muscles in her grief. The urge to lash out at him reared up again, her fingers clenching and trying to form claws. In the impulse-suppressing pause, she searched Agent 97's face again for signs of understanding and got none. That moment had passed.

She let out a ragged sigh and turned back towards the magical rose bush. They stood that way a long time, side by side, agent and friend, neither willing to break the vigil just yet, each mind racing to guess what the other would do. Enemies bound together by wonder at the sinister miracle they'd witnessed.

It was Agent 97 who moved first.

He replaced his sunglasses as slowly and carefully as he'd removed them. Reshielded, he tilted his head towards Sofi and nodded to her once in acknowledgment. Then, he turned on his heel and strode purposefully out of the cave on well-oiled bearings, leaving the disheveled bear-girl to grieve over her departed friend and her magical roses.

As far as he was concerned, this case was closed.

It's a darkness human eyes weren't meant to see. But I'm not afraid.

I float further downstream, weightless and drifting along the top of the black velvet river, buoyed on my rose-petal raft. Swirling currents of ghostly light lap my edges. The dancing waves rush through every sparkling cell of my skin until I laugh with the effort of containing so much pure sensation. No more fury or shame or guilt to sink me to the bottom, down to the clinging mud where I used to hide. Just the sheer exhilarating scent of utter, unbounded, unrelenting ease. I smile even though no one can see it, just because it feels so good.

And I dream, wrapped in a cracked-open heart filled with the ripest of roses. Finally feeling, finally happy, finally free.

Acknowledgements

In many ways, I have the book itself to thank first and foremost. It's the product of both a bizarre imagination and a personal dare. I started it on a whim for National Novel Writing Month 2012 at a time when my life was falling apart and I should've been doing anything but attempting to write my first piece of fiction since high school. But doing so gave me new focus, rekindled my fire for storytelling, and pulled me out of the darkness when I could've wallowed for years.

Thank you so much to my beta readers: Melissa Dominic, Will Laymance, Katy Rose, Kyeli Smith, and Jennifer Wilding. You read this book when it was shitty and didn't run away screaming when I cried about what you said, bless your little hearts.

Thank you also to the Professional Writer Types who consistently give me the inspiration I need to write something more than an angsty blog post: Sir Terry Pratchett, Francesca Lia Block, and Dianne Sylvan. Whether you know it or not, you've changed my life with your work.

Extra special thanks to my husband, Lino, who held me when I cried, told me I didn't suck, and reminded me that I write because I love to tell stories. I couldn't ask for a better partner.

And thanks to you, the awesome person reading this. This isn't a happy story. It's dark and emotional and strange. Definitely not for everyone. But if you ever got goosebumps in a tense moment or teared up with love or giggled at a pop-culture reference, this book is for you. Cheers.

Made in the USA
Charleston, SC
24 February 2013